PAPERGIRL

PAPERGIRL

Melinda McCracken
with Penelope Jackson

Roseway Publishing
an imprint of Fernwood Publishing
Halifax & Winnipeg

Copy editing: Brenda Conroy
Cover design: Andrew Lodwick
Printed and bound in Canada

Published by Roseway Publishing
an imprint of Fernwood Publishing
32 Oceanvista Lane, Black Point, Nova Scotia, B0J 1B0
and 748 Broadway Avenue, Winnipeg, Manitoba, R3G 0X3
www.fernwoodpublishing.ca/roseway

Fernwood Publishing Company Limited gratefully acknowledges the
financial support of the Government of Canada through the Canada Book Fund,
the Canada Council for the Arts, the Province of Nova Scotia
and the Province of Manitoba for our publishing program.

Library and Archives Canada Cataloguing in Publication

Title: Papergirl / by Melinda McCracken with Penelope Jackson.
Names: McCracken, Melinda, 1940-2002, author. | Jackson, Penelope,
1980- author.
Identifiers: Canadiana (print) 20190048506 | Canadiana (ebook)
20190048611 | ISBN 9781773631295
(softcover) | ISBN 9781773631301 (EPUB) | ISBN 9781773631318 (Kindle)
Classification: LCC PS8625.C72 P37 2019 | DDC C813/.6—dc23

FOREWORD

I was young when my mother wrote *Papergirl,* and I didn't think to ask her why exactly she wrote this story. She passed some sixteen years ago now, so there's no way to know for sure. Her life and times, however, contain some clues.

A creative person, Melinda received a music scholarship to go to university, graduated with an English degree and went to England to study as a visual artist. While there she wrote a biweekly column for the *Winnipeg Free Press* entitled "Melinda McCracken's letters from England." In one, she described a new popular musical act, The Beatles, to those back home!

Her formative years were spent in Montreal and Toronto in the countercultural 1960s, when many young people questioned the establishment values of their parents, the war in Vietnam and the problems of capitalism and patriarchy. Melinda was one of the voices of this new generation of hippies. She wrote about music and the arts and from a "woman's lib" perspective.

She became a mother in the early 1970s and returned to Winnipeg several years later. Seeing Winnipeg with new eyes and countercultural thought, I imagine she became interested in a major event in her hometown's history: the 1919 Winnipeg General Strike. She decided to write a fictional feminist story set during this pivotal event in local and international history. As a mother of a young girl, she wrote the story for children like me, her daughter.

I remember her writing *Papergirl* on her typewriter in the early 1980s, both in the little red house by the water at the Lake of the Woods and in the basement of our house in Riverview. She and my grandmother talked about what it was like to live in the early 20th century: ice delivered by horse for the icebox and the joys of homemade biscuits. And they also discussed the hardships many experienced during the strike. Melinda's story was completed but never published.

The manuscript was dug out of the archives and is being published to help celebrate the 100th anniversary of the Winnipeg General Strike. Through the eyes of Cassie, we experience the risk and promise of working people's collective struggle for a better future.

A huge thank you to Penelope Jackson for editing and enhancing the story. It is improved thanks to your thoughtful contributions. Thank you to Dennis Lewycky, Jim Naylor and Doug Smith for providing historical accuracy. Thank you Brock Brown for creating a teacher's guide. Thank you to the University of Manitoba Archives and Special Collections for housing Melinda McCracken's fonds.

Thank you to Wayne Antony and Roseway Publishing for bringing this story for all to read.

Melinda would have been proud to be part of the events acknowledging the 100th anniversary of the strike and people's enduring struggle for justice, peace and freedom.

Molly McCracken

CHAPTER 1

Tuesday, May 6, 1919

It had been a long, hard winter, and though the snow had been gone almost two weeks now, you could still see the occasional dirty patch in shady corners. The sun was finally warm on Cassie's face, but the ground was still brown and bare, and there were no leaves on the trees. Cassie always marked the change between winter and spring by the sound of horses' hooves. In the winter, they went *squeak-squeak* and the harnesses jingled with bells, but when spring came, the bells were put away and the hooves made a clean *clop-clop* sound. There was clopping coming from nearby Portage Street.

"Look, Mary!" exclaimed Cassie.

Her best friend looked to where Cassie was pointing.

"Crocuses! That's our fourth patch this spring. They're so late this year," Mary said. The girls always kept count of the signs of spring together.

"Better late than never," said Cassie. "And I definitely

thought it might be never this year."

The girls opened the wooden gate at the Hopkins family home, a small frame house on Langside Street in Winnipeg. Langside ran all the way from near the river to Notre Dame Avenue, but Cassie lived on the part that was just off Portage Avenue, the main street where all the department stores, banks, and office buildings were. Cassie's house was squashed fairly tightly against the house next to it, where elderly Mrs. Watson lived with her equally old tomcat, Rodney. The front porch of Cassie's house took up most of the front yard, and the shed took up most of the back. But still there was enough space for Cassie's family to plant a row of flowers in the front and a square of vegetables out back when summer came. There was also room enough for a robin, all by himself, to land and peck by the front steps for a worm.

"That's three robins now! And our first worm!" Mary paused. "Does the worm count if it's just been eaten?"

Cassie, whose full name was Catherine Hopkins, was ten and a half that spring of 1919. She and Mary were in Grade 5 at Carlton School, which was behind Eaton's department store at Hargrave and Portage. Carlton School was for children who lived downtown, like Cassie and Mary. Most of them were poor, or working class, also like the two friends. But some of them came from big houses down by the Assiniboine River, near the new Legislative Building, a few blocks south of Portage Avenue. Their fathers were doctors, lawyers, and businessmen. Cassie didn't like the wealthy children very much. They acted so superior, like they were smarter and better than the working-class kids, and the teachers always seemed to agree, playing favourites with the richest children. They always looked clean and never had runny noses or dirty faces. It was as if they were born clean. And they never wanted to play baseball or marbles with the other children.

Mary lived farther north on Langside, near Notre Dame Avenue. Mary and her mother didn't have a whole house. They lived in a small apartment without a back yard at all. Mary loved helping Cassie's family with their garden.

Cassie's father, David Hopkins, was a police officer, and so was her nineteen-year-old brother, Billy. With two men in blue in the house, Cassie and her mother felt well protected. Mr. and Mrs. Hopkins and Billy had come from England before Cassie was born. Everybody in the family had an English accent except Cassie, although Billy was losing his. In the wintertime, the house always seemed very full. Both Billy and Mr. Hopkins wore big fur coats made out of buffalo hides because it got very cold in Winnipeg, and police officers spent a lot of time outside. They also wore big, furry hats, so when they took off their coats and hats and hung them on the hooks by the back door, it was almost as if there were two extra people in the house. Mr. Hopkins worked in the North End Police Station, and Billy, being young and hardy, directed traffic at the corner of Portage and Main, Winnipeg's biggest intersection.

Once, when her mother was taking Cassie to the doctor, Cassie saw Billy directing traffic in his buffalo coat. He looked like a big teddy bear leading an orchestra. He loved his job, though, and was proud to be following in his father's footsteps.

Billy and Mr. Hopkins had put away their buffalo coats with summer coming. Now they wore high helmets, which Mr. Hopkins said were the same as the ones worn by the police in his hometown of London. They also wore blue jackets with a row of shiny buttons down the front, blue trousers, lace-up boots, and swirling capes that made them look very dashing.

Everybody in Cassie's family came home for their big dinner at noon, and Cassie usually brought Mary with her. The girls had from twelve till two for dinner, and Mary's mother was at work all day in a factory. It was much nicer for Mary to come and have a hot meal with the Hopkinses than to go home to her drafty flat to try to scrape together whatever food she could find.

Mrs. Hopkins stayed home and did the laundry, cleaned the house, and baked. For their big daily dinner, she would cook beef and cabbage, or sometimes chicken or fish, with a dessert like rice pudding or bread pudding or some of her preserves, which she put up in the autumn and kept in the cellar cupboard. The Hopkins family used a gas stove and had recently bought an icebox, which kept food cold with a block of ice in the top compartment. The ice was delivered by a man from the Arctic Ice Company, whose wagon was pulled by a large horse. He was an expert at chopping off just the right sized piece of ice and he would carry it dripping over his shoulder with big black tongs. While he was stowing it in the icebox, the horse, who was held back by a weight on a leather strap, made manure in the middle of the street. There was *always* manure in the middle of the street. "Horse buns," the kids called it. They were so used to the smell they barely noticed it.

Before they bought the icebox, Mrs. Hopkins had kept food in the cellar. They still stored all their potatoes, parsnips, beets, and turnips down there in the dark where they would keep, but with the new icebox, they could keep milk and eggs for several days without them going bad. They also had an indoor toilet — which not many of their neighbours had. Cassie did not miss scurrying to the frigid outhouse during the bone-freezing Winnipeg winters.

Cassie knew her family was lucky; she only had to look at Mary and her mother, Mrs. Smith. Mary's father had gone to fight in the Great War in 1915 and had been killed the following year. Since his death, Mary and Mrs. Smith had become even poorer. They received a tiny pension, but nowhere near enough to let them stay in their old house. They'd moved to a grim flat that had no icebox, no cellar, certainly no indoor toilet. That's why Mary's mother had to work so much, but even working fourteen hours every single day except Sunday, Mrs. Smith always looked hungry. Tired, too. Mary kept offering to stop school and find work herself, but her mother wouldn't hear of it. Mary still had to do most of the cooking and cleaning at her house — when there was anything to cook. And so she came home with Cassie for dinner.

"We've not much to spare, but a few good meals a week might keep that girl alive," Mrs. Hopkins would say.

The Great War had been terrible for many more than just Mary's family, Cassie knew. Billy and her parents discussed the war around the dinner table, and from their expressions and the tone of their voices, she had decided it was the most serious thing in the world. Millions of people had been killed, and many more millions had been injured. A lot of police officers had gone to fight in the war, and some, including many of Mr. Hopkins's friends, had died. But Cassie's father had a gammy leg, which he'd received in a scuffle with a criminal on the job. He worked at a desk now and wasn't eligible to fight in the war. Billy had been too young to go.

With the war over, thousands of soldiers had returned to Winnipeg to look for work. Some of them had been badly injured. The soldiers had been expecting to be welcomed like heroes, but they couldn't find jobs. Most people who had jobs didn't have enough to live on. Some men made only fifty dollars a month. Women who worked for the telephone company made fifteen dollars a week, and Mary's mother and other women working in factories made only seven dollars every week. And prices had gone up very fast. Eggs, bacon, shoes, clothing, beef, and coal were all very expensive. Billy said that prices were going up because the men who controlled the money pushed them up to get richer.

Yes, life was sad sometimes, Cassie had learned. But the warmth of the sun on her cheeks and the softness of the wind and the company of her best friend made her feel happy and hopeful. There was a small lilac bush in the

Hopkinses' front yard, and in a few weeks the lilacs would be out. They only lasted a week or so on the tree, but they had the loveliest smell. Lilacs always marked the time for Cassie when spring turned into summer. Soon she could take off her stockings and boots and wear her socks and shoes.

Cassie banged the gate shut, and she and Mary went around the path to the back door. Their boots were dry, but still they wiped them on the mat. Mrs. Hopkins liked her linoleum floors to stay clean, and Cassie knew she'd get it if they tramped in mud. They took off their coats and hung them on a hook. Cassie flipped up her braids, straightened the collar of her middy, and squeezed into her place at the oilcloth-covered kitchen table. Mary sat down next to her.

"Hello, girls," Mrs. Hopkins said. "How was the morning?"

"It was good. It's a lovely day out, Mum," Cassie said happily. "Spring makes me so hungry. What's for dins?"

"Stew," her mother answered as she stood by the stove, stirring a steaming pot with a wooden spoon. "And I had time to make a batch of fresh biscuits."

Mary and Cassie exchanged grins. Mrs. Hopkins's biscuits were legendary.

Just then, Mr. Hopkins came in the back door, swinging his cape from his shoulders onto a hook and tipping his helmet on top of it. He undid his brass buttons, took off his jacket, and sat down, taking his napkin from beside his fork and tucking it into the collar of his blue shirt. He smoothed his big moustache with his fingers, giving the ends a twirl.

"Dinner, me love," he said heartily, then sniffed the air. "Ahh, stew and biscuits. The way to a man's heart." He winked at her.

Cassie giggled. Mr. Hopkins frowned at her.

"As for you, young ladies, don't I recall some arithmetic test?"

"Yes, Papa," Cassie answered. She really didn't want to talk about it.

"Well?"

Cassie sighed. "I couldn't help it. I had an error." Cassie glared at the pattern in the oilcloth and wrote an O in it with the handle of her spoon.

"Now, now," cautioned Mr. Hopkins. "Nobody's perfect."

"I almost was. So close."

Mary snorted. "One error out of a hundred questions, Cassie! I only got 92, so what does that make me?"

"That's not what I mean," said Cassie. "It's that Barbara MacKenzie. She got them all right, as usual, and then stuck her tongue out at me when I didn't. Miss Parker didn't notice, or pretended not to. You know the teachers are just easier on the rich kids. Barbara came late to class twice this last month and Miss Parker didn't say anything! No lines, no detention, and if I so much as breathe too loud the teacher's mad at me. Big surprise Barbara got perfect on another test."

"Oh, hush, Cassie. You and Mary both did fine," said Mrs. Hopkins as she set a bowl of hot stew before each of them. "We won't wait for Billy."

Cassie stuck her nose in the steam rising from the bowl,

calming down immediately. The stew smelled rich and meaty. She watched her mother's plump arm put a heaping plate of fresh biscuits in the middle of the table. Then Mrs. Hopkins ladled some stew into her own bowl and sat down at her place.

"What's keeping him?" asked Mr. Hopkins.

"It's this strike. He's so involved. Land sakes, I hope he don't lose his head."

"He does love excitement, don't he, Mum?" said Cassie. She reached for the fresh biscuits and passed one to Mary. They were lightly browned on top and flaky and smelled good.

"Doesn't, Cassie, doesn't," Mrs. Hopkins corrected.

"But Mum, you just said ..." Cassie looked around the table. There was something missing. "Where's the butter?"

"It's still in the icebox, Cassie. I made a decision this morning. Butter's gone way up in price. We have to ration it and only have it on our toast in the morning. We can't afford more."

"Oh, Ruth, there you go, economizing. We've got to have butter." Mr. Hopkins dipped his biscuit in the gravy of his stew, and took a large bite.

"Not at today's prices," said Mrs. Hopkins sternly. "Why, it's not even the middle of the month yet and I'm running short of grocery money, even with Billy paying room and board. The way prices have shot up. You can always use bacon drippings on your bread, David. If I can find the pennies for the bacon."

The screen door slammed and Billy, dark haired and

rosy cheeked, flung off his cloak the way his dad had, then dropped his helmet over it.

"Prices, did you say?" he asked, rubbing his hands together and sitting down at his place. Mrs. Hopkins leaped to her feet to get him a bowl of stew. He was the apple of her eye, her only son. Fortunately, Cassie loved him too. "Prices are up eighty percent since the war started. Not wages, though."

"What d'you hear on the strike, son?" asked Mr. Hopkins. "By the way, your mother's rationing the butter. She's decided we can only have it with breakfast from now on."

"What, now butter?" Billy rolled his eyes to the ceiling. "It's big business. It's their fault I can't have a bit of butter on my biscuit."

"Percy at the station says it's the fault of the working man. He says prices go up because workers want better wages," said Mr. Hopkins.

"Wages have gone up eighteen percent, but prices have gone up eighty percent," countered Billy. "Do you think that's fair? The big boys make big profits. The only way is to organize for a decent wage. Let people get paid enough to live on. Anyway, in the end better wages are better for business. What will they do when no one can afford to buy anything anymore?"

Cassie saw Mary nodding. She knew all about the problems with wages, watching her mother slave away for a pittance. Cassie's family had been talking about the unfairness in Winnipeg for a year or so, too, although lately their conversations had an uneasy edge to them.

Cassie thought a minute, running her biscuit around the edge of her dish to scoop up the remaining gravy. "So, what's organizing got to do with it?"

"Well, one person alone can't make anybody do anything. He doesn't have much power. But thousands of people together, all demanding the same thing, and refusing to work till they get it— well, they might get it."

"The news, son, the news," Mr. Hopkins insisted.

"Well," Billy began, "ever since the Ironmasters went out on the first of May —"

"Where to?" asked Cassie.

"What? Oh. I mean they went out on strike. They refuse to work until they get higher wages and shorter hours."

"But how're they going to earn money? How're they going to eat?" This was the first Cassie had heard of the Ironmasters striking.

"Shh, don't interrupt," Mr. Hopkins ordered.

"No, no, that's a good question, Cassie. It's good to be concerned. It's true, if workers stop working, they stop making a wage. It makes it hard to stand up to the business owners. That's why we need to do it, though; so that everyone gets paid more in the end. It might not be so bad. Maybe everybody will get together and help. There's a lot of support." Billy had an excited gleam in his eye. "In fact, everybody might strike all at once. A general strike."

Mr. Hopkins started.

"A general strike. Is that like a general store?" Cassie snickered.

"You're a general disgrace," Billy said. "A four-star general disgrace." He reached over and tried to tickle Cassie, but she wriggled away. She passed her empty stew bowl to her mother. "What's for dessert, Mum?"

"The very last of my stewed plums." Mrs. Hopkins beamed. Cassie looked at Billy and made a face. "Ecch," she said.

"You don't know how lucky you are, miss," scolded her mother. "Why, there are people starving in Asia, and you turn your nose up at my plums. The very idea!"

"We may be starving ourselves in a couple of weeks," said Billy cheerfully. "I'm really looking forward to it. Nothing to eat. Nothing to eat at all. Think of it, Cassie. Absolutely nothing."

Cassie shot him a meaningful look. He glanced Mary's way and then cleared his throat, looking embarrassed. He'd forgotten how poor some other families in Winnipeg already were.

Cassie turned her attention to the bowl of stewed plums that had found their way under her nose. It was just the skin she didn't like. Why couldn't her mother peel the plums before she cooked them? With a sigh she dug in, carefully separating the skin from the plum proper, and making a pile of skins on one side of the bowl. Mary had no such hang-ups and was happily devouring her bowlful and listening intently.

Billy swallowed and went on. "Anyway, the men already on strike went to the council for all the unions, and the council got their members to vote on whether to have a general strike or not. So they voted today, and do you know, hardly anyone voted against it.'"

Mr. Hopkins looked pale. "We're in for it, mates. Blimey. And what about the police?"

"We voted a hundred and forty-nine to eleven to support the strike."

"Cor. So we'll be off the job too."

"What'll the city do for protection?" asked Mrs. Hopkins anxiously. "Gracious, I had no idea it was so serious."

"Yeah, Billy," said Cassie. "People will steal, and bad men will murder people and nobody will help them. All the policemen will be at home playing checkers. Ooh, I hope the school strikes too. Then I could go out and play ball. There are some books I've been meaning to read, too. Oh, I hope the teachers strike. Will they?"

"Hold your horses," said Billy. "First of all, the people in charge of the strike are pretty smart, although the businessmen try to make them look stupid. Do you think they'll let the city go without any police? They're smarter than that. If they do, the city could impose martial law."

"What's marshmallow law and where can I get some?" asked Cassie. She was polishing off her stewed plums. She had to admit, the juice was delicious. She scraped the bottom of her dish with her spoon. Her mother had warned her never to pick up her dish and drink out of it.

"Martial law," said Billy, ignoring Cassie's attempt at a joke, "means that the soldiers or the Royal North-West Mounted Police will be in charge and give the orders. So the strike committee, the people in charge, will likely ask us policemen to keep working through the strike, to keep everyone safe. But everybody is supporting it. Bakers, blacksmiths, firemen, sleeping car porters, all kinds of people in low-paying jobs. Richer people will probably still go to work. But I don't know how they'll reach their offices if all the elevator operators are out."

"They'll have to walk up!" cried Cassie. Then she asked, "Will we have to go to school? That's all I want to know."

"Well, the schools will probably stay open. The teachers aren't unionized, and they work for the government."

"Oh, now," Mrs. Hopkins tutted. "You don't want to miss school anyway, do you? You want to get perfect on your next test. What about beating Barbara MacKenzie?"

"Ah, she's not so smart," said Cassie, her confidence renewed now that her belly was full.

"She's pretty smart, Cassie," said Mary, but she didn't look very playful.

"I guess." Cassie thought for a minute. "But Billy, Barbara MacKenzie will still be there after the strike. I don't want to miss out on a holiday. Will it be fun? Will it be exciting?"

"Well, it'll probably be exciting, but —" said Billy.

"Cassie, dear," interrupted Mrs. Hopkins, "a general strike is very serious business. It is not fun. The whole city will shut down. We won't be able to phone. We might not have lights, or water, or ice, or gas. Oh, David." She looked at Mr. Hopkins as the seriousness of the situation dawned on her. "We'll use up all our savings. What are we going to eat?"

Mr. Hopkins looked down at his empty bowl.

"Now, now, Mum," said Billy, patting his mother's arm. "Not to worry. There'll be plenty to eat. Everybody will pitch in and help, because everybody will be in the same boat. Don't you worry now."

But Mrs. Hopkins bit her lip and twisted her hands tightly together. Cassie didn't like it when her mother got worried. It made her feel a little scared, not as safe as she usually felt.

Suddenly, Mary jumped up and ran to the back door, pulling her jacket on.

"Mary, where are you going?" asked Cassie.

"We'll be late for school," Mary said.

"Well, wait for me and I'll —"

But Mary opened the door and ran out of the house, calling, "Thank you for dinner, Mrs. Hopkins," over her shoulder.

Cassie turned to her parents as she rose from the table.

"That was odd. She never leaves without clearing her dishes. Or without me!" She looked at the clock ticking away on the kitchen wall. It said ten minutes to two. "I guess she's right to rush, though." She gulped down the last of her milk, wiped her milk moustache off with the back of her hand, and set her dishes on the counter. She quickly put on her jacket and dashed out, letting the screen door bang behind her.

CHAPTER 2

When Cassie got back to school — just in time — Mary wasn't there. Maybe she wasn't feeling well, Cassie thought, hoping it wasn't the flu. It had been a month since anyone in their school got sick with the terrible Spanish Influenza, which had killed so many people that winter.

Cassie found it hard to concentrate, knowing how much was happening. She wanted to tell all her classmates about the general strike ahead, but every time she turned toward someone, her teacher noticed and glared at her till she put her eyes back on her work. Miss Parker was used to Cassie and Mary trying to chat all the way through class. She often said they were two peas in a pod, but not in a cheerful way, the way Cassie's mother said it. She seemed to expect the worst from the girls and sometimes seemed disappointed at their high marks. She adored Barbara and her friends, always asking them to clean the blackboard and praising their handwriting. She usually followed this up with a pointed glare at Cassie — whose cursive writing, to be fair, was a little lacking.

It wasn't that Cassie didn't like learning. It's just that class was so boring compared to what she could be doing — gardening, listening to her parents, fishing, riding the streetcars around the city when Billy was willing take them. Last summer, she and Mary had had freedom as soon as their chores were done. Cassie would finish her own, then go help Mary with all of hers, and then they'd spend all afternoon roaming the streets of their neighbourhood and beyond.

When the bell finally rang and Cassie was free to go, she walked to Mary's place instead of going straight home. She opened the front door, which hung a little crookedly in its frame, climbed the rickety stairs to Mary's flat, and knocked. It took a while before Mary came to the door, and when she did, her eyes were puffy and her nose was red.

Cassie took a step back. "Oh ... are you feeling ill? Do you need me to get my mum?"

Mary shook her head. "I'm not sick."

"Well, where were you, then? Miss Parker wasn't pleased you were gone."

Mary's eyes welled up and she took her ragged hanky out of her sleeve to wipe them. "I'm so worried. My mum and I can barely afford to eat and live as it is. What if her factory goes on strike? What will we do?" She began sobbing, which from the looks of her was about the twentieth time that afternoon.

Cassie pulled her friend to her and gave her a big hug. "I'm not sure what anyone will do. But we'll figure it out, okay? You know we'll always share whatever we have with you, and with your mum too, if she needs it. We can cut each potato into six."

Mary gave a small laugh.

"Besides …" Cassie pulled back and looked into Mary's eyes. "We might get to miss school."

* * *

On the morning of Thursday, May 15, Cassie could barely sit still. At breakfast, Billy had told her that today was the day.

"Mark my words, we're going to change this city once and for all," he'd said around a mouthful of toast. "Those fat cats won't know what to do with themselves!"

Sure enough, at just past eleven, Principal Milne came to the door and asked to speak to Miss Parker in the hallway for a moment. The students were on edge and began to whisper to each other. Cassie whirled around and mouthed to Mary, just behind her, "It's happening!"

Mary smiled, but still looked worried.

When Miss Parker came back into class, she cleared her throat. "Class, as you may have guessed, the strike committee has called a general strike. You may speak with your families about it at dinnertime, but for now, we will continue with our compositions." There was a collective groan from the class, who could barely stand not to go see what was happening outside.

"Bunch of Bolshies," came a voice from the back of the room. Miss Parker glared at the class and they quieted down, but not happily.

Cassie knew that voice. Barbara MacKenzie. *Of course* she didn't want the strike to happen — her father was a fancy lawyer, and his clients wouldn't be making any money to pay him without workers doing their bidding.

The clock inched its way towards noon, and even before the bell rang, the children were out of their desks, jamming through the doors, most cheering and running down the hallways out the front door of the school. Cassie waited for Mary at the front steps, and together they raced towards Portage Avenue to see what was going on. Despite her worries, Mary's face was as flushed with excitement as everyone else's.

The streets were as they'd never seen them before. They were full of people — people who usually worked. Boys and girls and men and women came pouring out of the buildings and into the street. Everybody was walking; the streetcars had stopped running. Everyone looked happy, as if they were just beginning a long vacation.

"I bet the bosses are mad," said Mary. "It would take a lot of nerve to stop working when your boss didn't want you to." Her colour faded a little. "I should go see if my mum's home."

* * *

The first night of the strike, Cassie lay in her little bed in her room upstairs. Her mind was going sixty miles a minute and the air was full of electricity. Cassie could hear her mother and father talking quietly downstairs. Billy was away at yet another meeting. Usually, if she lay very still and held her breath, she could hear almost everything her mother and father said to one another. And she usually tried so hard to be silent that she'd fall asleep long before this. But her eyes were wide open. She had to go back to school tomorrow, too. She wondered if there was any way she could get out of school while the strike was still on. She hoped they wouldn't stop the strike before she'd been able to really experience it.

Often in the evenings, Mrs. Hopkins would either do some knitting or darn Mr. Hopkins's socks so they would last a few more months. (Whenever Cassie saw her father with his boots off and a toe coming through his black socks, she'd sing, "Mr. White is out of jail again," and Mrs. Hopkins would get very upset and start looking for her sewing basket.) Mr. and Mrs. Hopkins would sit by the fireplace in the parlour. Mr. Hopkins would relax and smoke his pipe, with his shirtsleeves rolled up, his collar unbuttoned, and his suspenders hanging down around his waist. And Mrs. Hopkins would mend and mend. Sometimes, she turned the collars and cuffs of her husband's and son's shirts so that the worn part would be inside where nobody could see it. Sometimes she patched sheets, but those she usually sewed on her treadle sewing machine.

Tonight, Cassie could hear the crinkle of the newspaper Mr. Hopkins was reading. He puffed on his pipe, his puffs getting shorter and puffier and angrier as he read. He crackled the paper, turning page after page, and finally there came a big sound as he then tossed it down in disgust.

"I don't know what to make of it, Ruth," he said. "The

paper's got it all wrong. They say the strikers are trying to start a revolution, to overthrow the government and cause violence and bloodshed, burn down houses, kill people. Now, we know that isn't true. Blimey, they're even calling us Bolshies. Bolshevists are Russian revolutionaries, I know that much. But we're not Russian, and we're not revolutionaries. We just want peace and quiet and honest work for enough money to keep us going."

"I don't want to have to take in laundry," said Mrs. Hopkins, tugging at her yarn. "I'm not so sure this strike's a good thing. What, I ask you, is everybody going to eat? There are *twenty-five thousand* people striking. With no money, there's no food. What will *we* eat, for goodness' sake?"

"Surely we have enough vegetables stowed away in the cellar to last us for a week," said Mr. Hopkins. "And there's always oatmeal, we have plenty of that. Don't fret, luvvy; it'll be all right."

"If the strike goes over a week, we'll be just as badly off as everybody else."

"It never will. Stop your worrying."

Cassie could feel herself starting to worry too. So she did what she sometimes did in the evening, and crept from her bed. Silently, she crossed her little room and opened the door, then snuck to the very top of the stairs and sat where she could spy on her parents through the open parlour door. Sitting here, she could hear her parents much more clearly.

She watched as her mother snipped the yarn with her

21

sewing scissors. Then Mrs. Hopkins held her darning needle up to the light, squinting at it with one eye as she put the yarn through it. She started in darning again, holding the wooden darning foot under the hole in the sock to have a surface to weave the yarn against.

"If we don't have enough to eat, we'll get sick. Sure thing, I've seen that happen — think of all those poor souls with the Spanish flu. And when you're sick, you can't work, and there's no money."

"I'm not worried, Ruth. Do you see me worrying? Billy's out getting all worked up, while I'm content to sit at home of a night with the missus, reading the paper. Except the paper's wrong! Blast! What's a man to do? I need something to occupy my mind."

"You can always read the Bible," Mrs. Hopkins said.

Mr. Hopkins turned at the sound of the back door opening. Billy came in and began talking before he'd even taken his hat off.

"I've just been to a meeting of the returned soldiers. The leaders of their organizations tried to get them to stand against the strikers. But they decided they were *for* the strikers and would do their darnedest to preserve law and order! It's grand. There are about ten thousand of them. Their support means a lot."

"What else?" Mr. Hopkins asked eagerly.

"Well, the printers are all going on strike tomorrow, so there won't be any newspapers. The Citizens' Committee of One Thousand won't be able to print any more lies for a few days at least."

"The Citizens of … whatsit?"

"The businessmen against the strike. The bosses and the men with money. Anyways, from what I hear, the newspapers have scared the rich people in the South End so much that they're frightened to sleep in their own homes. They're going to sleep in churches. Apparently, people down east think that Winnipeg is having a revolution. They think the streets are running with blood, and all that. They got that from the big newspapers."

"Well, what about us?" asked Mrs. Hopkins. "Can't we tell our side of the story?"

"Well," Billy continued, "the strike committee is planning to set things straight by publishing its own paper, a strike bulletin. Volunteers are going to write it and print it without pay. They think they can get one out by Saturday night. They'll cost a nickel on the streets."

The grownups paused, but Cassie could see her mother still looking worried.

"Will we have water and light?"

"Oh, the waterworks won't be cut off. They've been asked to keep the pressure up. And the lights will be on. I think they'll get milk to the children, too. No one wants complete chaos. But I'm worried about the Citizens' Committee of One Thousand. They're very powerful and ruthless. They're headed by a lawyer named Andrews. They're going to act for the federal government, go right over the heads of the Winnipeg and Manitoba governments."

"All the way to Ottawa? Why, they've never paid any attention to us before."

"Well," Billy went on, "there's a rumour that the Canadian government is trying to get a loan of a hundred million dollars from Wall Street in New York. And Wall Street wants the government to stop this 'revolution' in Winnipeg before they hand over the money. That's why Ottawa is taking an interest."

"Well, I'll be," exclaimed Mr. Hopkins. He shook his head. "Hard to believe, hard to believe."

"Do you know anything about how people are expected to eat, Billy?" said Mrs. Hopkins. *She's certainly concerned with food*, thought Cassie. "I'd offer to help if I thought there was anything I could do. But we'll run out of supplies faster than I want to think of it."

"I think they're making some plans," said Billy. "There might be something you could do."

Cassie could see her mother finishing up her mending, so she silently rose and walked back into her bedroom, softly closing the door behind her. She snuggled into her bed. If her mother, father, and brother were all helping with the strike, there must be some way she could help too.

CHAPTER 3

Seven days later, on Thursday, May 22, after the strike had been going on for about a week, the *Free Press* began publishing again. Mr. Hopkins had a fit reading their headlines about "anarchists and aliens" leading the strike and how all the strikers were Bolshevist revolutionaries.

Cassie was getting used to seeing Portage Avenue full of people in the daytime, strolling up and down in the sunshine. In a way, everyone seemed happy to be free of work, as they usually worked such long hours.

The school was still open, though. This bothered Cassie. It would have been such a perfect time for a holiday, right at the end of such a long winter. The last time schools were closed was in the fall, when the flu had spread like wildfire through the city. That had been frightening, not fun. Now there was more excitement and anticipation in the air. Some of the kids had begun to play hooky — mostly the poorer kids from the north end. In class since the strike started, the usual tension between the rich children and the poor was even higher than normal. Even fewer kids showed up on Wednesday and Thursday.

Cassie asked Mary a few times how she was doing and whether she and her mother had enough to eat, but Mary wasn't giving her straight answers. Cassie's family had had to stop buying beef and pork, but they still had enough chicken, cheese, eggs, potatoes and other vegetables that they weren't going hungry. Cassie had been able to convince Mary to come over to visit on the weekend, so she was getting at least one square meal a day. Cassie hadn't seen Mrs. Smith, though, and couldn't imagine she had much of anything to eat.

Billy came home Thursday at suppertime with some news. Mary was over, and Mrs. Hopkins was serving a roast chicken with potatoes and carrots, heavier than their usual suppers, but Billy had been unable to come home for dinner.

Cassie knew nobody had expected the strike to go on this long, but here it was a week later and it was no closer to being settled. The Citizens' Committee of One Thousand and the strike committee hadn't even gotten together to talk at all.

"What's going on then, Billy?" Mr. Hopkins asked after he said grace.

"Honestly, you won't believe it. You know Honourable Arthur Meighen?"

"Of course," said Mr. Hopkins, at the same time as Cassie said, "Who?"

Billy looked at her. "He's the Minister of the Interior, and he's the acting Minister of Justice, too. Well, he and Senator Gideon Robertson — that's the Minister of Labour — got on a train in Ottawa bound for Winnipeg."

"People got on a train? That's not news, Billy."

Mary cracked a smile.

"Oh, hush up, Cassie, will you. At Fort William, two men from the Citizens' Committee of One Thousand got on the train with them." Billy paused so everyone could take in the significance. "And then, outside of Winnipeg, two *more* men from the Citizens' Committee boarded the train." Billy sat back triumphantly, as though he'd just figured out the secret to everlasting life.

Mr. Hopkins cleared his throat. "Couldn't it be a coincidence?"

"Not a chance. The Citizens' Committee is linked with the federal government. I bet you Meighen and Robertson heard about the so-called Bolshevist revolution in Winnipeg and believed every word. They haven't bothered to be in touch with the labourers at all, mind — the Minister of Labour, no less! I don't know what they're up to here, but I don't like it one bit."

Mary spoke up. "Do you think they'll end the strike and get people working again?"

"No one knows what they'll do, Mary. Not yet."

Mrs. Hopkins reached over and patted Mary's hand kindly. "Now, dear, I'm sure your mother will be back to work in no time."

"But not before we've got fair wages for everyone!" protested Billy.

Mrs. Hopkins shot him a dark look and he quieted down.

Once supper was over, Cassie asked if she could walk Mary home. As the two girls wandered the busy blocks up to Mary's place, they marvelled at the crowds around them.

"It's odd seeing all these people out, isn't it?" said Mary. "It's odd having my mum home, too. She's getting a lot of sleep, finally, but …"

"But there's nothing to eat?" said Cassie.

Mary nodded slowly, reluctant to admit it.

"We can have her over for dinner tomorrow," Cassie said. "Just bring her over and say my parents want to talk about the strike with her."

Mary's brow furrowed. "I honestly don't know if she'd let you give her any food, Cassie. She's accepted no help since Papa died, and I doubt she'll start now."

"Let me try," Cassie said as they climbed the peeling steps to Mary's building. On the second floor Mary opened her apartment door.

"Mama? Cassie's here with me," Mary said.

Cassie stepped inside the cold flat. It was one room, with two cots in one corner, a small kitchen along the opposite wall, and a table and two chairs. Spotlessly clean as always, the flat nevertheless felt desolate. Cassie, whose family didn't have much, felt sick at how little money Mary's mother made, no matter how hard she worked.

Mary's mother was sitting at the table, staring out the window. It was true, she looked more rested than usual, but her cheeks were more sunken than ever.

"Oh, hello, girls," she said, turning and smiling warmly

at her daughter and Cassie. "It's lovely to see you, Cassie; it's been too long."

"Hi, Mrs. Smith. I was just walking Mary home, and I wanted to invite you for dinner tomorrow. My parents asked me to." The lie was easy to tell, as Cassie's parents were always hoping to do more for Mrs. Smith.

Mrs. Smith looked embarrassed. "Oh, now, that's not necessary, Cassie —"

"Billy wants to talk to you about the factory," Cassie lied again. "Research, for the strike committee. They want to get some more perspectives for the speeches and the bulletin and everything. So it would be really helpful if you'd come over."

Mary was looking at Cassie in awe, as though she hadn't known how smoothly her friend could spin a tale. But it worked. Mrs. Smith's embarrassed expression had eased.

"Oh, I see. Yes, all right, Cassie. Please tell your parents thank you, and I'll see them tomorrow."

As Cassie walked home alone, she felt triumphant that her ruse had worked, but sick that there was nothing more that could be done for Mrs. Smith. She thought about what Billy had told her, about the Canadian government being on the side of the Citizens' Committee of One Thousand. How *could* they be? They must not know about people like Mrs. Smith — a hardworking woman whose husband had died in the war, who worked all hours of the day and could barely feed herself and her daughter, let alone put enough away for leaner times. Someone needed to tell the real stories, so the rest of the country would know it wasn't Bolshevists revolting in Winnipeg, but everyday hungry people. It was so frustrating to be just a girl stuck in school, where she'd never be able to make a real difference.

* * *

As she predicted, Cassie's parents were happy to hear Mrs. Smith had accepted Cassie's invitation, although she didn't tell them how she'd managed to convince their guest to accept their hospitality. When Billy arrived for dinner, Cassie quickly pulled him aside and explained her white lie. Billy understood immediately.

"You're right, you know. I'd love to hear more about Mrs. Smith's work. I know those factory workers have it hard."

Soon Mary and Mrs. Smith arrived, and after everyone was sitting down, Cassie helped her mother serve a simple cabbage soup with biscuits and boiled eggs on the side.

"So lovely to see you, Anna," said Mrs. Hopkins to Mary's mother.

"Yes, we're very grateful that you've come over to talk to me," said Billy. Eager to distract Mrs. Smith from his parents' confused expressions, he spoke quickly. "We'd love to hear more about what it's like in the factories. It's important that all our workers are understood."

"Well, thank you for having me. The soup is wonderful."

"Tell them, Mama, about what it's like there."

Mrs. Smith set her spoon down. "I wouldn't want to complain, you understand. I'm grateful for the work. I don't know what I would've done without it, since ..."

There was a silence, though not an uncomfortable one. Since the war and the flu, everyone had either lost a loved one or knew someone who had. Cassie was used to the adults around her taking a moment to think about those who had died.

"Truly, I would rather be working right now. I prefer to keep busy, and … well, you know I need the pay."

"But wouldn't you rather be making a fair wage?" Billy broke in. "It's not right how workers are treated."

Mrs. Smith nodded slowly. "I see what you mean, Billy, but I don't know that it's my battle to fight. I need to keep food on the table. I need to make sure Mary has what she needs to grow." She paused. "I can't pretend the factory is a nice place to work. Many days, I don't see the sunshine, and I barely make enough for us to get by. The work is hard on my back and my eyes, and we don't get enough breaks to stretch out the parts that start hurting. I see why everyone wants this strike. And, you know, it may even hold some opportunities for me. The phone operators have left their jobs, and the phone company wants to keep the lines open. They want volunteers, and anyone who shows an aptitude might be employed after all this mess is over."

Billy looked horrified. "But you can't be a scab! We need to stick together!"

"Simmer down, son," Mr. Hopkins said sternly. "We all know where you stand, and where I stand. But you can't tell me you don't understand why someone would feel desperate enough to be a scab."

Cassie was confused. "What's … what do you mean, a

scab?" She touched her elbow gingerly, where a scab had formed over a scrape.

"It means a dirty strike breaker, someone who works for the employers while the rest of us protest, someone who ruins the strike for everyone else!" said Billy.

"Billy, that's *enough*," said Mrs. Hopkins. "Anna, I'm so sorry. I wish there were a way to make this easier on everyone. It's a hard situation all around."

Mary spoke up suddenly. "There *is* a way. There's a food kitchen for women. And they're helping women with rent, too. Mama, you just need to start accepting help."

Mrs. Hopkins looked surprised. "Is this true, Billy?"

He nodded. "Yes, Helen Armstrong, the head of the Women's Labour League, has started a kitchen to feed women and girls. Men, too, if they have good reason or they can pay. But mainly for the women."

"There's a woman organizing it?" Cassie asked. So far, Billy had only mentioned men working on the strike committee and leading initiatives.

"Yes, down at the Strathcona Hotel. It's called the Labour Café."

Cassie knew the Strathcona, which wasn't too far from their house.

Mrs. Smith and Mary exchanged a long look. Cassie wondered if they were feeling the same glimmer of hope that she was.

CHAPTER 4

Sunday, May 25, 1919

The weather was growing warmer and warmer. The leaves were out. It was lilac time. Mary and Cassie had lost count of signs of spring; the whole world was bursting with life.

Cassie walked with Billy to Victoria Park on Sunday afternoon after dinner. The strikers had church services in the park, two blocks from City Hall on Main Street. They called the services the Labour Church. To Cassie, the enormous crowd just looked like a sea of hats. There were the men's peaked caps, felt hats, and a few summer straw boaters crowded into the little park, with women's wide-brimmed hats and the children in smaller version of the adults' hats. Five thousand people were present to hear the Reverend William Ivens, known as Ivens the Terrible. Cassie was too short to see over the multitude of hats, so Billy hoisted her to his shoulders.

Reverend Ivens called out, "The Citizens' Committee

says you must call off the sympathetic strikes. What is your answer?"

Five thousand men and women shouted, "No!" They were speaking for the other strikers not present, whose ranks had now swelled to thirty thousand. Billy was thrilled at the numbers.

Reverend Ivens told the crowd that that very afternoon, Senator Robertson had called a meeting of the postal workers, who were employed by the Canadian government. At his meeting, Robertson ordered all the post office workers to be at work at ten the next morning, or else they would be fired, lose their pensions, and never be hired by the Canadian government again. Cassie felt a stirring when Reverend Ivens spoke — a strange feeling that she was connected with everyone here.

Lawrence Pickup announced that the postal workers had voted not to go back to work, and everyone applauded and cheered. A hat was passed to collect money to feed the girl strikers at the Labour Café.

When Billy and Cassie got home, Mrs. Hopkins was bubbling with excitement.

"I've got a lot to do!" she told them. "I've been to see the Women's Labour League at the Strathcona. They have a big dining room and kitchen and they're going to feed all the striking girls from the department stores, laundries, clothing factories, candy factories, hotels, and restaurants. Without the café they'd be starving. They're also being given money to pay the rent on their rooms. Some of the strikers are offering girls rooms in their homes for free, but

I don't think we have the space here."

"What will the men do?" asked Cassie.

"Oh, the meals are for men too. Men without money can get tickets from the relief committee and eat. Why, they're serving fifteen hundred meals a day from the Strathcona! All for free!" exclaimed Mrs. Hopkins, taking the hatpin out of her hat and setting her hat on the hall table. She fluffed up her hair and came into the kitchen where Billy and Cassie were sitting. "But there's some doubt as to how long they'll have the hotel. I don't think the owner approves of what they're doing."

"Of course he doesn't," said Billy. "He's a landlord; he'll be on the Citizens' Committee's side."

"Nevertheless," said Mrs. Hopkins firmly, "I start tomorrow. And do you know what? They say we can make up a batch of biscuits, *my* biscuits, to feed everybody. Imagine, me, serving my biscuits to fifteen hundred people. I never thought I'd live to see the day. Mind you," she added as an afterthought, "they probably taste better in small batches."

"You'll be famous!" cried Cassie. "You could start a biscuit business. I can see it now. Mum's Better Baking Powder Biscuits. Get 'Em While They're Hot!"

"Oh, don't be silly. My biscuits aren't that good. They're just biscuits. I don't want to turn into a businesswoman, anyway. That would be against my newfound principles."

"Mum," Cassie wondered, "if you're at the Strathcona Hotel, who's going to make *our* dinner?"

"Young lady," said Mrs. Hopkins firmly, "you and the boys will just have to fend for yourselves. Your father knows a bargain at the grocery store. And Billy can fry an egg. You'll make out. Those girls are hungrier than you are. Think of poor Mrs. Smith."

That got Cassie thinking. "Do they need any more volunteers?"

"Don't you even think about it. You've got school."

Cassie laughed. "Not me. Mrs. Smith. If they can help with her room and her food, couldn't she volunteer there, instead of being a scab? She did seem interested when Mary mentioned it."

Mrs. Hopkins looked thoughtful. "I know they could use more help. Why don't you run over and see if she's home, let her know she should join me in the kitchen tomorrow. If nothing else, she'll have some food in her."

"What about Mary? She's not striking; how will she eat?"

"There are some other girls your age helping. Perhaps she could come too, just to keep her fed while the strike is going on."

"What? How come she can skip school and I can't? Couldn't I come to the Strathcona too? Maybe they'll need somebody to peel potatoes. I'm good at that."

"You are?" Mrs. Hopkins raised her eyebrows.

"Well, uh … what I mean is, everybody's doing something but me. There must be something I could do. There *must* be."

"Are you sure you just don't want to play hooky?" her mother asked sternly.

But it wasn't that. Well … it was that a little. But Cassie could also see the hunger growing in the people around her. She could sense the monumental unfairness of life in Winnipeg, how different life was for the rich and the poor. She wanted to keep families like hers and Mary's healthy and happy and well paid for their hard work.

"Say, I've got it!" said Billy, snapping his fingers. "Of course! It'd probably be harder than peeling potatoes in some ways, but a lot more fun ..."

"What have you got up your sleeve?" Mrs. Hopkins asked suspiciously.

"Well, they're looking for people to sell the strike bulletin on the street. It's a really important and responsible job, Cassie, because that bulletin brings all the news to the strikers. They need somebody for my corner, Portage and Main. They had a boy, but he has to stay home and help his family. I could keep an eye on you."

"Hmmph," said Mrs. Hopkins. "That's no job for a girl. She'd be better off underfoot with me than running around as a paperboy."

But Cassie loved the idea. "Oh, please, Mum, please. If I don't like it, then I'll come and help you. It sounds so exciting. Portage and Main! And think, with the strike bulletin, everyone will know the truth that's not getting reported in the newspapers."

"Most of the people will be friendly," added Billy, "but you may have to keep an eye out for rich kids."

Cassie's eyes narrowed. What were they doing on the streets?

"There's a gang of them," Billy continued. "They've pushed around some of our helpers. No grownup would touch a little girl, but those boys ... And then there's Freddy. You'll get to know him, I expect."

"I know I can do this," said Cassie, before he said so much her mother would never let her do it. "I can help. When can I start?"

"We need someone straight away. Tomorrow, if you can."

"I don't know about this," Mrs. Hopkins said. "But ... oh, I guess if you're nearby, Billy, there's no harm done."

Cassie could hardly wait to tell Mary her mother would be working in the kitchen; she knew it would help convince Mrs. Smith. She ran to Mary's house to let them know. On the way over, she thought again about what Billy had told her. One thing intrigued her.

Who was this Freddy?

CHAPTER 5

The relief had been clear on Mrs. Smith's face when Cassie proposed she work at the Labour Café alongside Mrs. Hopkins. Early the next morning, Mary and her mother arrived to meet up with Cassie's mother and walk over to the Strathcona together. Mary and Cassie exchanged a quick hug and wished each other luck at their new positions — and shared a little quiet glee at missing school.

"Promise me no matter how tired out you are, we'll meet tonight so you can tell me everything!" said Mary.

"Me? Tired? No chance. And I want to hear all about the kitchen, too. I'll see you tonight," said Cassie.

Cassie ran to the James Street Labour Temple to pick up her papers, which had been left just inside the door for all the paperboys and the one papergirl. Feeling very important indeed, she made her way through the streets to the corner of Portage and Main. Along with her pile of papers, she carried a rock to keep her papers from blowing away and a sandwich. She wore a little leather pouch on a belt around her waist filled with change to give customers.

She was proud and ecstatic at finally being free, but to her surprise, she was also a little afraid. This was her very first job, and she was being trusted with real money and with the message of the strikers. She wondered if she could do it.

When she got to the corner where she was planning to stand, she noticed somebody already there. He was in the best spot, where all the people were passing by. He had several piles of papers around him with rocks holding them down.

Cassie stood and looked at him, wondering what to do. Had she misunderstood Billy? Was this boy already passing out the strike bulletin?

He was about two years older than her, wearing a peaked cap like all the boys, a white shirt with the sleeves rolled up, and knickers. His face was dirty, and underneath the dirt he was a little pale. There were dark circles under his eyes. The peak of his cap was worn in one place, and she saw him tug at it a couple of times — probably the habit that caused the wear. His ears stuck out, and Cassie could see the dirt behind them, as well as the smudges inside his open collar. And to top it all off, there was a homemade cigarette dangling from his mouth. He kept it in the corner of his mouth as if by magic or some special glue, as he held his paper up and bawled at the top of his lungs, "GET-cher PAY-per HEE-ar! READ ALL ABOUT IT!"

Hmm. He looked poor, so he should be on the side of the labourers, but could that be a newspaper he was selling? Cassie got a bit closer and saw that it was indeed the *Tribune*.

He continued yelling, "Reds want revolution! Agitators loose in city! Send the aliens back!"

Cassie was shocked. She knew there were many who opposed the strike, but not the poor people who knew how unfair things were.

The boy stopped for a minute and looked at Cassie with her armload of papers. He took the cigarette out of his mouth and stubbed it on the sidewalk with his boot. She noticed there was a hole in the toe of his boot and he didn't have any socks.

She stood there, unsure what to do, squinting into the sun. A man patted her on the shoulder. "Say, little girl, can I have a bulletin?" He held up a nickel.

Cassie remembered the important job she was meant to be doing.

"Uh ... 'scuse me, sir ... sorry." She scrambled to pull out a single paper from the pile, almost dropping them all. She decided to put down her rock first, then took the man's nickel. She stole a glance at the boy. He was glaring at her with his hand on his hip.

After the man left, the boy said, "Hey, kid. You, with the Bolshie news. This is my turf. Now beat it."

"This is your what?" asked Cassie politely.

"Turf. Territory. This is my corner, dummy, can't you see? How'm I gonna sell my papers with you hangin' around with the enemy rag?"

"What are you selling?" asked Cassie.

"The *big* paper. The *real* paper. GET-cher PAY-per HEE-ar!" he yelled.

He sounds like a hungry calf, thought Cassie, giggling to herself. Then she straightened up. "Hey!" she said. "You sell the Citizens' Committee paper, I sell the strikers' paper. There's no competition 'cause they're two different stories."

"Not on yer life, kid. Now beat it."

Cassie wasn't about to give any ground. If she messed this up, she might be taken off the task altogether and sent back to school, while Mary had all the adventures. She stomped her foot.

"I *won't* beat it. I have as much right to this corner as you have. This is public property in a free country!" She thought of telling him about Billy, her policeman brother nearby, but Billy always told her to fight her own battles.

"Look, kid, you don't have to own a corner to *own* it. I've been here for two years, and nobody is going to tell me to move."

"Well nobody's going to tell me to move either, so there."

"Move?" he yelled. "You haven't even started standing anywhere yet." He put down his papers and walked up to Cassie. He was a few inches taller than she was, and when she looked up into his hard little eyes, she was a bit afraid. "Now see here, whatever-your-name-is ..."

"It's Cassie. Cassie Hopkins."

"Just see here, you. This is my corner. You don't even have to sell papers; you probably think it's some kind of lark. Well, I work every day here. When it rains, I'm here. When it snows, I'm here. When the wind blows like a screaming banshee and turns my guts to icicles, I'm here. I don't sell papers for fun, or because I'm a goody-goody. I sell papers for money. To get money. To eat."

"What about school? What about your parents?" Cassie blurted out, and immediately she could have kicked herself. She knew how many parents had died in the last few years, between the war and the flu.

"I don't go to school anymore. That stopped when my old man got sick. He worked seventy-seven hours a week in a factory. Made sixteen dollars a week. Think that was enough for us? His health gave out and there's seven of us kids in the family. My mother gets sick a lot too. Specially in winter, she gets to coughing and all that. I had a little baby sister, she died last year. Pneumonia." He had slowed his speech and looked off in the distance. Then, as if remembering where he was, he shook himself and continued. "This corner is very, *very* important. I fought for it and I won it. I got my customers coming every day. They know where to find me. I got to be here. And I ain't movin' for no Bolshie like you."

Cassie felt sympathetic. His story was undeniably familiar to her — and it even made Mary's life look easy by comparison. At least Mary was getting an education.

But she was puzzled, too. Of all people, this boy should have been standing with the strikers, demanding a better deal for all the workers in Winnipeg who were suffering, like his father, and yet he was calling her names. She couldn't understand it. She thought she shouldn't ask any more questions. Maybe she could be his friend instead of his enemy.

"All right," said Cassie. "I understand better now. I won't

invade your corner. You can have it. Tell me where I should stand. What's your name, anyway?"

"Frederick S. Wolchinsky. Freddy for short," he said grudgingly.

So *this* was Freddy.

"What is the *S* for?"

"Stanislawo. Like Stanley. It's Ukrainian." He said this last part like a challenge.

An immigrant. Selling papers that called him an alien. Poor Freddy, thought Cassie. Just as her mum always said, you think you're badly off 'cause you've got no shoes, till you meet somebody who has no feet. This boy was so dependent on the money from his job, so afraid of losing it, that he had to take the side of the very people who were hurting him.

"Okay. Hi, Freddy. Tell me where I can stand."

"Let's see. Go about twenty feet farther back. Keep goin'. Keep goin'. Now stop. You can sell your papers there. I don't think we'll have no conflict."

"Maybe people will buy both papers," she called to him. She wondered if you could be on both sides at once.

"Both of 'em?" said Freddy incredulously. He was losing his toughness in spite of himself. "Listen, if people buy both of 'em, they got more money than sense. GET-cher PAY-per HEE-ar!"

Cassie admired his pluck despite his bad fortune. His cap was at a jaunty angle, and he was tough and hardworking.

Cassie thought she'd better yell too. But what? She cleared her throat and began. "STEE-rike PAY-per!" No, that wasn't quite right. "Stee-RIKE PAY-per." Better. People started to buy the bulletin, and she was in business.

The sun was getting hot. Cassie noticed Freddy had a jar of water. He stopped and took at drink. He saw her looking at him.

"Want some?"

Cassie nodded. He walked over and she took a long drink.

"Don't take it all, greedy," he said. "Next time, you should bring your own." He winked at her and walked back to his corner. He sat down on the sidewalk cross-legged and started to roll a cigarette.

"What do you smoke those awful things for?" called Cassie.

"Taste good," Freddy called back. "I roll my own because I can't afford tailor-mades. And once you start" — he shrugged — "you can't stop."

"Well, why'd you start?" Her voice was starting to get sore and she wandered a little closer to him.

"Oh, wanted to feel like a big shot, I guess. Ain't nothin' like 'em for relaxin'."

Cassie made a face. "My mum says they're bad for you. Stunt your growth."

"Yeah, and bread crusts give you curly hair." Freddy gave a dry laugh that turned into a cough. "Say, Cassie, what you want to be when you grow up?"

"I'm not sure yet, but maybe a typewriter girl. I don't want to get married right away. I'd like to be out in the world, that is if I can get the training."

"Know what I want to be? I want to be the boss. The Big Boss. I want to sit up there in one of them buildings in a big office with my feet on the desk and smoke a big cigar. I want to drive a big car, so people will look up at me and say, 'There goes Mr. Frederick S. Wilson.' Have to change my name, of course, so people won't know I'm Ukrainian. People don't like Ukrainians. Rich people don't, anyway. Maybe I'll own a newspaper or something. Then I could hire you. You could be a reporter. How about that? A girl reporter."

Cassie smiled; she was pretty sure those didn't exist. Then she stretched her neck to look up to the big stone cornices and windows and ledges that rose endlessly above her. It was a long way up. The buildings were very tall. She wondered how Freddy could even imagine himself up there. She wondered if he'd live long enough to see the day. With all his problems, she couldn't quite see him in a suit with his feet up on the desk, the Big Man smoking the Big Cigar. That would probably be the MacKenzies. This wasn't a world where the Freddies could become Big Men. Cassie wondered if it could ever be.

CHAPTER 6

When Billy came to let her know it was time to go, Cassie was tired out after all, but she'd sold all but two of the bulletins.

"Good job, squirt," said Billy. "It seems like you handled old Freddy pretty well, too."

"I guess," said Cassie. "He's not as bad as he seemed at first."

They were rounding the corner to their house when Cassie spotted Mary and their mothers approaching from the other direction. Despite her tired feet, Cassie ran to meet them.

"Well?" she asked. "How was it?"

All three answered at once: "Wonderful!"

They laughed.

"I'll tell you what, they seemed to like my biscuits," said Mrs. Hopkins, beaming. "I'll go in and get supper on — just for today, mind. We've been run off our feet. Mary and Anna, you're welcome to stay, although as you know it will be quite simple fare."

Mrs. Smith shook her head. "No, no. We'll be just fine. We both had a big dinner. Thank you, though. And thank you for the invitation to work with you today." She turned to her daughter. "Mary, you can tell Cassie about your day, and then come right home, you hear? We'll have another long day tomorrow."

As she walked away, Mary turned to Cassie. Her eyes were sparkling. "Cassie, it really was wonderful. There were so many girls there that we got to feed, who wouldn't have food otherwise. I was mostly in the kitchen scrubbing dishes, but I got to hear all the grownups talking. I even saw Mrs. Armstrong!"

"Who?" said Cassie.

"Mrs. Armstrong! You know, the leader of the Women's Labour League? She's helped a lot of the girls unionize. She was right there! She smiled at me! I've never met a woman like her. I didn't know there *were* women like her. And she was so kind to my mother. She took her aside to ask if we have enough money for the flat. I think she saw how skinny Mama is and was worrying about her."

It gave Cassie a thrill to imagine a woman having so much authority.

"What about you?" asked Mary. "How was it being a real live paperboy?"

"Paper*girl*, thank you very much. And it was … interesting. My throat hurts a little from all the shouting, but I met so many people who are on our side." She paused. "And I met one who really, really isn't."

"Ooh, a fat cat walking by? I hope you gave him heck."

"Nothing like that, or maybe I would've. No, there was a boy there selling the newspaper, but it didn't make sense to me, really. He's an immigrant from a very poor family that he's supporting just with his wages. Neither of his parents can work, but he's selling that awful paper full of lies and calling out the terrible things it reports. I know he needs the money, but I don't know why he doesn't realize that this strike is for people exactly like him."

Mary scowled. "Sounds like a fool. Keep your distance from traitors like him."

Cassie laughed. "Why, you're becoming quite the radical! Just one day with this Mrs. Armstrong and you're a proper Red, aren't you?"

Mrs. Hopkins opened the front door and called, "Cassie, I need you to come in and do the sweeping, please."

"No rest for the working girl," said Cassie happily to Mary. "Maybe I'll see you tomorrow morning again? I missed you all day."

"I missed you too," said Mary. "I'd better get home. I'm so tired!"

Tired though she may have been, Cassie saw her best friend skip a few times as she walked away up the street.

* * *

Cassie was out on the street every day the strike bulletin was published — which was every single day. She began to feel at home on the street after just a few days, calling out to pedestrians, talking to them, selling them papers. She wasn't sure she understood what the papers said yet. But she definitely understood how important the strike bulletin was, because as soon as she brought her papers to the corner, people flocked to her like pigeons around someone with a bag of breadcrumbs.

Some people didn't have nickels, just quarters, so Cassie had to make change. Sometimes when she ran out of change, she would ask Freddy for some. If they both ran out at the same time, Cassie kept an eye on Freddy's papers while he dashed into the nearby CV Cafe for nickels.

People soon got to know her, and would say, "Good morning, Cassie. How's business today?" and "How many papers have you sold today?" A few times men driving horse-drawn wagons stopped for a moment at the curb and leant out for Cassie to sell them a strike bulletin. On Thursday, a horse turned around and nipped her arm as she handed its driver his change. She was more afraid of the frisky horses than she was of any of the rich kids Billy had warned her about. She felt perfectly safe with her brother directing traffic not a hundred yards away. It was easy to see why the police had decided to keep working; if Billy ever left his spot in the middle of the intersection, the cars and wagons could get in an awful mess.

On the morning of Friday, May 30, it was terribly windy. Cassie tried to hold her skirt down with one hand and sell papers with the other. Her hair was coming loose and blowing in wisps around her face, which was getting browner every day she stood out in the sun. The bulletin she held up said:

WHAT WE WANT

The Demands of the Strikers are:

1. The Right of Collective Bargaining
2. A Living Wage
3. Reinstatement of All Strikers

WHAT WE DO NOT WANT

1. Revolution
2. Dictatorship
3. Disorder

Freddy had gone for change, but he was taking a long time to come back. Cassie was handing out papers to all the reaching hands holding nickels, then suddenly noticed hands reaching out to her without any money in them. She looked up and found herself surrounded by boys in peaked tweed caps like Freddy's and suits with vests, like little grownups. They seemed to want to paw at her. Cassie pulled away, frightened.

"Look at her!" they taunted. "Look at the papergirl! Thinks she's a boy!"

"Yeah, have you heard her holler?" A boy mimicked her in a high dainty girlish falsetto, "Paper, mister, here's a pretty, itty-bitty paper for you!"

"Bet your dad's a Red," another boy said. "Bet you're one of the Bolshies."

"He is not!" Cassie protested. Her voice was so high it almost squeaked. She realized she was scared. "My dad's a policeman! He's protecting you!"

"Ha!" said an especially tall, thin boy who seemed bolder than the others. Cassie looked up at his face and her stomach sank. Of all the people to come by — this was Barbara MacKenzie's older brother, Nick. He had a reputation at school for being a terrible snob and a bully. "My dad says that even the police are Red in Winnipeg." Nick opened his jacket and stuck his thumbs in the armholes of his vest. "Your dad's either a Red or an alien. My dad says the government's going to throw all the aliens out of the country."

"My dad is not an alien!" Cassie shouted.

"Sure he is. I bet he eats perogies, reeks of garlic, and he no spikka da Inglish too good. My dad says the aliens want to start a revolution."

"My dad is British!"

"Oho!" said all the boys at once, trading knowing looks.

"British, hm? So what does Nick the Stick think about Brits? Tell us, Nick, can Brits be trusted?"

"If he's a Brit, he could be an anarchist or an agitator. Or a socialist. Oh, any number of terrible things," said Nick the Stick.

"My dad is NOT terrible! How dare you!" screamed Cassie, sticking out her chin. With one eye, she looked across to see if Billy had noticed she was surrounded, but he was too busy, and the blustery winds were probably drowning out the sound of her voice. She wondered how defiant she should get.

"Listen," growled Nick the Stick. "My old man is a big shot in the Committee of One Thousand."

Cassie knew that well enough. Nick clearly didn't

recognize her as his sister's rival, though.

He continued, "My dad and his friends are letting you sell those papers out of the goodness of their hearts. Let's see one of those, anyway." He grabbed a paper from Cassie's hand and held it up for his friends to see. They all pressed in to read it. "'What we want — A living wage,'" Nick read in a sneering voice. "As if they're not already getting too much! 'What we do not want. Revolution. Dictatorship. Disorder.' Hah! That's *exactly* what they want! They want to take over! Well, Miss Brit, your strike is worth just as much as this!" He took the rock off Cassie's pile of carefully folded papers and kicked them over, and the wind took the whole lot of them and whirled them along the street, so that they clung to people's legs and got trodden underfoot by horses' hooves. A draft carried them up towards the corniced buildings above, where they floated and soared like gulls over the river.

"Get those back! Those are important!" Cassie yelled, tears in her eyes. The papers floated off down the street, whirling around with the dust. One flattened itself over a well-dressed man's face. He plucked it off, and when saw what it was, he made a disgusted face and then crumpled the paper into a ball and threw it away. Cassie ran after the papers, trying to catch them, and she could hear the boys' laughter following her. She gave up trying to chase the papers and turned back to the group of boys.

"See that bluecoat?" she roared, livid with rage. Cassie was using her ultimate weapon. "He's not a Red! He's my big brother!" She pointed at Billy, who just then finally noticed what was happening. He halted traffic in both directions and began to run to her rescue. The boys' eyes widened. Sympathetic strikers nearby had started to pick up the crumpled papers for Cassie. She wasn't afraid anymore.

"Let's get out of here!" cried Nick the Stick. The boys raced away into the crowded street, bumping against people who turned and watched them disappear. Some people came up to Cassie and offered her the crumpled papers, but they were beyond reading. Cassie sat down on the sidewalk with her chin in her hands as Billy approached.

"Guess I'm too late, eh? You hurt?" She shook her head. All the traffic was waiting, motors running, horses pawing the pavement. "Sorry, Cass. Got to get back. Talk later!" He ran back to his position and waved the Main Street traffic through.

Freddy sauntered up, hands in his pockets.

"And where have *you* been?" Cassie asked angrily.

"Had a soda," he said blithely. "Why? Something wrong?"

"Something *wrong*? I'll say. I just lost practically all my papers because of your rich bosses' snotty kids. I bet I lost five dollars' worth."

"That's what happens to people who rock the boat," said Freddie, grinning. "They get pushed around by people who're stronger. That's why I always toe the line. Yes sir, no sir, right away sir. Besides ..." Freddy's voice dropped to a whisper. "D'y'know what they'd do to me if they found out I was the dreaded alien? Beat me into a pulp, that's what. Dry me up and blow me away. So I'm quiet. Verr-rry quiet. And

Nick the Stick don't bother me none." He patted Cassie on the shoulder. "Chin up, kid."

As he strolled back to his spot to sell papers, Cassie glared at him. He knew it was Nick the Stick bothering her — that meant he'd seen the whole thing and stayed inside on purpose. And she thought they'd become friends, or at least friendly. She picked up her rock and walked forlornly home.

The house was so quiet with her mother out working. Cassie sat down at the kitchen table and opened her little purse. Eleven nickels and one quarter. That made eighty cents, or sixteen papers. And she'd started out with a hundred papers. She owed the strike committee four dollars and twenty cents. Not much less than a whole day's wages for her father.

She felt as though her stomach was eating her heart. She'd never be able to pay all this money back. The strikers had trusted her and she'd let them down.

Suddenly she heard the click of the back door opening and her mother rushed in.

"Oh, my dear girl. What happened? Tell me everything."

"What are you doing here?" Cassie's heart was lifting just seeing her mother. Mrs. Hopkins bustled to get Cassie a glass of milk while she answered.

"A boy, a skinny little thing, came running to the café saying there was an emergency for a Mrs. Hopkins. I couldn't believe it, of course, but he said you were all right but that I was needed at home. Someone had sent him … Frankie? Teddy?"

Freddy had sent someone to get her mother? Right after throwing her to the wolves?

"Anyway, Mrs. Armstrong said I could come right home. You must tell me what happened."

Cassie took a drink of milk. It was off, a bit warm. She grimaced and then told her mother of the morning's events. As she was finishing, Billy rushed in, out of breath.

"I got somebody to stand in for me to lead the traffic orchestra," he said. "I was too late. I'm so sorry, Cassie. How much did you lose?"

"Four dollars and twenty cents' worth." Cassie sat glumly staring at the floor. It was awful to be in debt. "They'll never let me sell the strike bulletin again."

"Oh, come on," chided Billy, lifting up her chin so that her brown eyes looked straight into his blue ones. "It's not the end of the world. The strike committee doesn't have a heart of stone. And unfortunately, this isn't the first time this has happened. They'll know it's not your fault."

"What?" said Mrs. Hopkins. "You said our Cassie would be perfectly safe selling the bulletin. Now you say it's dangerous?"

"It's not exactly dangerous. Cassie, those boys didn't hurt you, did they?"

"No. And I'm not afraid of them." Cassie straightened her shoulders. "They just made me furious, that's all! All those good papers, all that work by the strike committee. Ruined. Think of all the people who might've bought the bulletin today and found out what was happening. Now they won't know! It was an important one, too. Letting people know that we aren't trying to have a revolution, that all we want is fairness."

"I know," said Mrs. Hopkins. "I read a copy in the café. Which, by the way, you're about to start working at."

"But —"

"No. I won't hear another word. You do not belong on the streets, it's not safe. You can come chop onions and sweep the floors along with Mary, or you can go back to school."

Cassie sat as tall as she could, trying desperately to seem mature. She spoke as evenly as she could. "I know the café does important work, and I'm so glad you and Mary and her mother are working there. But I've gotten so good at selling the bulletin this week, you know I have. The customers know me! And the paper is how we can convince everyone in Winnipeg and all over the country that we're striking for the right reasons. Please, please let me keep selling it."

"It's my fault more than the streets," interrupted Billy. "I should've been watching more closely. Cassie's been handling everything so well that I haven't been checking up on her enough. But I will, Mum, I promise. Give our papergirl a second chance, will you?"

Mrs. Hopkins's shoulders were slowly retreating from around her ears, and her face was a little less red than it had been. "One more chance," she said. "All right? One more. But I won't have my girl in a fray. I am proud of you, love. I know you're working hard; even Mrs. Armstrong has noticed. But if anything else happens, you're into the café with me and Mary."

Cassie nodded.

Billy's run home was catching up with him and he began dabbing the sweat off his forehead. "Mum, could I have a glass of milk too?" he said.

Mrs. Hopkins took the milk bottle out of the icebox and poured Billy a glass. He took a drink and frowned.

"It's warm!"

"The ice has melted. There's just a weeny piece left. Somebody'll have to go to the ice company with the wagon and get us a piece before the milk turns."

"I'll go." Cassie sighed. It was a long way, and she was so tired from the morning's dramatic events, but somebody had to do it.

She wondered what Nick the Stick was drinking right now. Nice cold milk? Rich people could pick up ice in their cars when there was no delivery.

"Warm milk," Billy said thoughtfully, staring at his full glass. "I don't like it. But if warm milk is the price of social justice, I'll happily pay it." He raised the glass to his lips, gulped the liquid down, then ran his tongue across his lip to lick off his milk moustache.

He clearly felt this was a very noble act, but he was just as clearly holding in a shudder at the warm milk. She didn't mention it. Instead, she asked, "What exactly does justice mean? The courts?"

"Ah. Justice. It's one of the most important things there is, Cassie. Some people think it doesn't exist. Have you ever heard anyone say there's no justice? 'There's no justice,' they say, and shake their heads. It just means they haven't experienced it. I believe you have to live it to know what justice means. When it happens to you, you know. You'll find out."

"When?"

"Well, you just never know." He got up, put on his helmet, and went out the door.

He really could be maddening.

Just as he went out, Mr. Hopkins, wearing street clothes, came in. He sat down heavily and wiped his brow with his handkerchief. It was getting warmer and warmer out.

"What did you find out at the meeting?" Mrs. Hopkins asked.

"Well," Mr. Hopkins heaved a great sigh, and winced as he straightened out his gammy leg. "I might not be working much longer after what happened today. The police commissioners — our bosses, Cassie — gave us an ultimatum. They said we had to swear not to take part in the strike. If we did, we'd be fired. So, do you know what the union did?"

"I bet I do!" cried Cassie, forgetting her own losses. "They said they wouldn't do it, didn't they?"

"Well, it kind of looks that way."

"Hooray!" cheered Cassie.

"Blimey, sometimes I think the union's got beans for brains. This strike is getting us bloody nowhere!

Mrs. Hopkins gasped. "David!" she exclaimed. "Don't swear!"

"I'll bloody well swear if I bloody well want to!" Mr. Hopkins was steaming. Cassie had never seen her father like this. There was definitely something wrong. "Everybody,

everybody thinks we've done a bloody fine job. But if we keep supporting the strikers, they'll force us off the streets and bring in the army. The whole force is calling it the Slave Pact. They say only a slave could sign it. I can't help it. I've tossed in my lot with the strikers. I may not be a copper in future, luvvy," he said, looking at Mrs. Hopkins.

"I'm with the strikers too!" cried Cassie. She felt a hot flush rise in her cheeks.

But her mother looked worried. "As long as no one's hurt," she said quietly. "You know, David, it's hard to believe how insensitive people can be. Do you know what happened this morning before I had to come home? The owner of the Strathcona Hotel came in, fancy as you please, right as we were starting to work for the day, and told us he doesn't want us to use his kitchen and dining room anymore. The Citizens' Committee is putting pressure on him. Mrs. Armstrong argued with him, told him how many girls we've been feeding and how many families we've been helping, but he just wouldn't change his mind. Told us we have to find another place. Well, Mrs. Armstrong thinks she's got the Oxford Hotel, which has an even bigger dining room, so he can take his kitchen and stick it where —" She seemed to notice Cassie was still there and stopped. After a pause, she brightened. "The Oxford is right near Portage and Main, convenient for everybody. Perhaps it'll all work out. I'll be able to keep an eye on our papergirl, anyway."

"Perhaps it'll work out," agreed Mr. Hopkins. "But truly, it doesn't look too hopeful. I don't think the Citizens' Committee wants to settle this strike at all. They're not getting together with the strike committee to work things out. They want to break the strike to crush us, to not give us anything at all, keep things exactly the same forever. Our grandchildren will be working themselves to the bone for no money too if the Citizens' Committee have their way. I'm sure of it."

After her experiences today, Cassie had to agree.

CHAPTER 7

The very next day, Cassie walked to Portage and Main with Mary. The Labour Café had moved overnight and was up and running already in the Oxford. Freddy seemed surprised to see Cassie with her pile of papers.

"Well, I'll be darned. If it isn't Miss Bolshie, back to face the music," he said in awe.

Cassie could feel Mary stiffen beside her.

"Yes it is, Mr. Alien," Cassie said airily.

"Sh!" whispered Freddy in alarm, looking over his shoulder. "You'll give me away."

"Not as much as sending a runner to get my mother might've," she said. "Thank you."

He shook his head and began sucking on the cigarette hanging out of his mouth. "Don't know what you're talking about."

"Did you hear about the police? They've been given twenty-four hours to decide whether to support the strike or not. If they do, whoops, no police. And that's what the Citizens' Committee of One Thousand wants. It wants to bring in the army."

"You're joking." He looked frightened. "The army! They kill people, you know. That's what soldiers are for, to keep people down. At least in my father's country, that's what —"

"Well, what on earth did you *think* was going to happen?" burst out Mary. Freddy's eyes widened as he took her in. "You're here supporting the bosses while workers are starving to fight for your rights! Yes, *your* rights. For the rights of *all* workers, even the ones betraying us. I couldn't believe it when Cassie told me about you, you little traitor. And standing aside while she was attacked yesterday. I hope the army *does* come, and take care of treacherous —"

She was interrupted by the sound of bagpipes and drums and feet marching. A huge parade was coming down Main Street, the Union Jack waving brightly at the front.

"Soldiers!" gasped Freddy. "Already, they're taking over the city!" He was poised to run. The thunder of marching feet moved nearer and nearer. Cassie could see the paraders clearly now. They weren't carrying guns. They weren't even in uniform.

She reached her hand over and stilled the quivering Freddy. Mary looked disdainfully at their contact. "Don't worry, Freddy," Cassie said. "I think these are the returned soldiers who support us. Support the strikers," she corrected herself quickly.

"Yes," said Mary. "Not *us*, hey, Freddy?" She walked away to the new Labour Café location without a glance behind her.

"Who on earth is that?" said Freddy.

"My best friend in the world," said Cassie. "She and her mother are all alone, and she wants this strike to work. I can't believe how little they have."

Freddy looked wryly at her. "Just she and her mother in the family to take care of? Oh, how difficult their lives sound."

Of course. It was so hard to talk to Freddy about anything; his family was destitute. Few had it worse than them. But he was so resolutely on — well, the wrong side.

The soldiers kept streaming by, marching along silently behind the flag. There must have been ten thousand of them.

"Where're you going?!" called Cassie to one of them as they passed.

"To the Legislature to see Premier Norris," he answered. "We're trying to help!"

She watched the soldiers march away, the wail of the bagpipes trailing a few blocks behind them.

* * *

With the café so close to her corner now, Cassie popped in for her midday dinner.

"You sure you don't want to switch sides and come eat some hot food?" Cassie had asked Freddy as she gathered her diminished stack of bulletins and left her spot.

Freddy looked wistful, but his words were resolute. "Yes. I'm sure. Have a good dinner."

When Cassie walked into the café, she was greeted by familiar scents of stew and, she was sure, her mother's tea biscuits. There were dozens of women there, eating around tables together, and a few men as well.

She smiled at the women greeting her and went over to the line to get her own bowl of food. Though her mother had been stretching their supplies as far as they could reach, Cassie had been feeling hungry all the time lately ("Get used to it," Billy had said. "I got hungry the day I turned ten and I didn't feel full till I was eighteen") and was looking forward to a hot meal in the middle of the day instead of her usual sandwich.

As she waited she learned that the soldiers had passed the headquarters of the Citizens' Committee of One Thousand, torn down their sign, and carried it along with them. There was an energy to everyone in the café — having the soldiers' solidarity meant so much.

When she got to the front of the line, she was delighted to see Mary serving up.

"Hello, ma'am," Cassie said playfully. "Might I have a bowl of stew?"

Mary smiled. "Why, yes, little miss," she said in a posh voice.

They couldn't chat; other hungry people were multiplying behind Cassie in line. But she winked at her friend and sat down nearby to watch her working.

There was a new confidence to Mary's movements. She looked so self-assured here, amongst all these workers united by a common cause. Cassie could remember being little with Mary, studying ants for hours in the summertime, having roaring snowball fights in the winter. She could still see the five-year-old in Mary, but today for the first time she thought she could see the future twenty-five-year-old, too.

At one point, a short, brown-haired woman with twinkling eyes walked out of the back kitchen and said a few words to Mary, patting her shoulder kindly. Cassie couldn't hear what she said, but she saw Mary's face light up. Once the woman had moved on, Mary looked over at Cassie and mouthed, "*Mrs. Armstrong!*"

Of course! This was the famous agitator who'd convinced so many women to unionize and who'd whipped this very kitchen into existence. She had a growing reputation in the city as a labour leader and an activist. She was one of only two women on the strike committee. Cassie's mother had a great deal of respect for her, even though she was so different from how women were supposed to behave.

Cassie watched Mrs. Armstrong make her way through the crowds of girls and women eating their food. She kept pausing to make sure people were all right, listening to them, and even hugging some who were tearful. Cassie felt more and more intrigued, especially once she could see Mrs. Armstrong was coming her way. Was she really going to speak to her?

"Ah, the papergirl!" said Mrs. Armstrong when she reached Cassie. "I saw you working out on the corner this morning. How brave of you to be standing with us when you're so young, especially after your spot of trouble yesterday. And your mother made these wonderful biscuits, didn't she?"

Cassie could only nod. Mrs. Armstrong seemed to sense her shyness. "No need to worry, dear. We're all sisters in this fight. You eat up and get back out there to spread the good word!" She tapped Cassie's stack of bulletins as she moved away.

Cassie felt flushed and excited and looked over at Mary to see if she'd caught the exchange. She had and beamed back at Cassie. Cassie finally understood what Mary had been going on about. Both Mrs. Hopkins and Mrs. Smith were strong, hardworking, and loving. But there was something different about Mrs. Armstrong. She was in charge, not just of her own house, but of so many other people.

She spotted Mrs. Smith in the kitchen when she was returning her plate. She had more colour and her cheeks were plumping up. She was talking with Mrs. Armstrong while she stirred a big pot of fragrant soup, and at one point she laughed aloud. Cassie realized she hadn't seen Mary's mother laugh for years, not since they'd gotten word about Mary's father. As hard as this strike was on everyone, it was clearly doing some good for Anna Smith. Cassie saw her own mother bustling past as well, holding a tray of her biscuits high over her head.

She left the café feeling even more resolute that the strikers knew the way of the future better than anyone else.

"What's got you so happy?" Freddy barked. "You Reds'll never win!"

Cassie just rolled her eyes and set to selling the bulletin as best as she could, chatting with her customers about the soldiers' march.

At the end of the day, walking home together, Mary was bubbling over.

"She told me I was doing a wonderful job and thanked me for missing school so I can help," Mary said. "She said she could see I have a bright future no matter what I do!"

Cassie smiled and took her friend's hand. "I don't doubt it in the least."

* * *

On Friday, June 6, Cassie read the strike bulletin aloud to Mary on their way to Portage and Main. "Strikers, hold your horses. This is the hour when you can win. Steady boys, steady. Keep quiet. Do nothing. Keep out of trouble. Don't carry weapons. Leave this to your enemies. Continue to prove you are the friends of law and order." Cassie said, "I wonder why everybody is supposed to be so creepy quiet."

"Think about it," said Mary. "All the Citizens' Committee wants is trouble. They're looking for an excuse to call in the army, and that would be the end of the strike."

Cassie eyed her friend. She and Mary were certainly getting an education, even if they were missing school to do it.

Mary raised her voice as she walked past Freddy. "The only way we'll have a fair shake is to work together, Cassie. And to overcome the bosses. And the traitors." She narrowed her eyes at Freddy and walked over to the café.

"Your friend sure has a problem with me," said Freddy.

"She just cares a lot. You should try it sometime," Cassie replied. But she wasn't grouchy about it. She'd come to appreciate Freddy's companionship on the street corner, even if she knew she couldn't rely on him for protection.

Without Billy standing nearby, she felt more exposed, and she worried that Nick and the other rich boys would realize she was alone and come back to bother her. Thank goodness the café was close enough to run to. She couldn't imagine Mrs. Armstrong letting any hooligans in there.

She didn't have long to stand imagining; she was still run off her feet with customers. She barely even had to yell to advertise the bulletin anymore. Everyone knew who the papergirl was and what she was selling.

* * *

That Sunday, as they had on every recent Sunday, Billy, Cassie, and Mary went to Victoria Park to the Labour Church. J.S. Woodsworth, who was helping with the strike and had written some of Billy's favourite essays about the workers, spoke. There were over ten thousand people there to listen — more than any other service yet — and they raised more than fifteen hundred dollars to help strikers' families eat and pay rent. Cassie knew from her family's own struggle and especially Mary's that every single penny would be put to work. Even the strikers who ate at the café were getting a hungry look about them. Cassie was sure that some of them didn't eat except for the noontime meals there.

When Labour Church finished, Cassie asked Mary if she'd like to come over. "You're welcome to, though my mum is tired out from working at the café so much."

Mary looked at her a bit funny. "Well, now you know

what it's like," she said. "Or a little, anyway. You know, my mother has *more* energy now that she's only working at the café and not locked away in the factory six days a week. I'm going to spend the rest of the day with her."

The friends hugged, and as Mary walked away, Cassie entered her house to find her father and Billy talking quietly in the parlour while her mother worked in the kitchen. Billy's hands were clenched, and he seemed like he was trying to stop himself from shouting. They stopped whispering once they noticed Cassie.

"What's the matter?" she asked.

"It's nothing," said her father at the same time as Billy said, "The Slave Pact, we're calling it. It's coming. They want to stop police from ever unionizing. The city will go to the army."

Cassie hesitated. She wanted to stay and find out more, but at the same time, she was beginning to be quite overwhelmed with all the details of the strike. She decided to go into the kitchen to help her mother. Everything had been so new for weeks; a little routine felt safe.

"I'll peel the potatoes, Mum."

Mrs. Hopkins looked up, startled. "Oh, you're home. Don't worry, dear. I'll do these."

"No, I want to," said Cassie. Her mother tried to stop her from pulling the potatoes over to herself, and when she saw them, she knew why. These were the dregs of the dregs, some with especially long pinkish white roots coming out of their eyes, some wrinkled, and some even slimy.

Cassie looked up at her mother, shocked. Could her

family really be running out of food? Not just the butter and the meat, but plain old potatoes too?

"They're all that's left. Just … try to cut off the bad parts."

Cassie hadn't realized it was this bad in their pantry. She tried to do as her mother said, but the sight and smell of those old potatoes almost made her sick to her stomach.

* * *

The next day, Cassie and Mary passed a few police officers who looked less at ease than usual. They knew them a bit because of Cassie's brother and father, and normally the police would wave or say hello, but the men they passed looked preoccupied. Even Billy, walking with the girls to his intersection, was subdued, though his convictions hadn't changed.

"None of it is our fault, you see. We've done our best to work with the Citizens' Committee, but they've just ignored and threatened us. We've no choice. They're backing us into a corner with this Slave Pact. I don't know, girls. I feel as though everyone's starting to run out of fight as they run out of food."

"Not me," said Mary. "But then, I might be better fed now than I was when my mother was working. That's not likely true for most people."

"Definitely not us," said Cassie, thinking about the potatoes last night.

Both Billy and Cassie were beginning to worry about things at home. Mr. Hopkins's spirits were sagging; the weather was turning even hotter and muggier, the lilacs had browned, and he suffered in the heat. And the Hopkinses were running out of food. Cassie could hardly believe it, but it was true. Her mother was worried, she knew. The potatoes, disgusting as they'd been, were now gone for good. They had finished the last of Mrs. Hopkins's preserves about a week ago. There was oatmeal, still — oatmeal for breakfast, oatmeal for supper, and oatmeal for Billy and Mr. Hopkins's midday meals, unless they ended up coming to the Labour Café too. Oatmeal without milk and sugar wasn't much to taste, but it was filling, at least. For now.

Something would have to change soon for this city to survive the strike.

Cassie and Mary left Billy at his intersection, and Mary walked into the Oxford Hotel to the café while Cassie set up in her spot with the bulletin. She waved to Freddy, who was already at his corner, smoking a cigarette.

"Why such a long face?" he called. "You look so serious."

"No reason," she said. He wouldn't understand. Well, that wasn't quite right — he'd understand all too well. She sighed, baffled once more at why his loyalty lay with the people who had left this hunger in her belly and his.

* * *

Back at the corner on Tuesday afternoon, Billy was even more tense. He'd heard that as constables were going off their beats, they were being taken into the chief's office and asked to sign the Slave Pact.

When his shift was wrapping up, he walked over to Cassie. "I'm off, then," he said. "Have you sold enough to leave? Want to walk to the station with me?"

Cassie only had a few bulletins left, so she quickly went to the café to let Mary know she wouldn't be walking home with her today, then went with Billy. Billy's pace was slow; he didn't want to go through with this.

"It's no good," he kept saying. "They're up to no good. They need us to keep the peace. It's like they don't even *want* peace."

Cassie wasn't sure what to say, so kept quiet. At the station, she waited outside while Billy went in.

He emerged a few minutes later, downcast and tense.

"Come on," said Cassie. "Let's get you home and I'll make you ... well, a bowl of oatmeal."

Mr. Hopkins was already home as well. "Take it you didn't sign, then?" he said to Billy.

"Of course not. No one will."

"Aye, I know. I didn't either, of course. By ten tonight the whole police force will be locked out. Think of it — none of us allowed to work, and this hungry city left without protection."

* * *

Billy offered to walk Mary and Cassie to work the next day, as he had nothing else to do. When Cassie picked up her strike bulletins to sell, the office was abuzz. She stopped a young man hurrying past and asked for the news.

"The police," he said. "They're out."

She nodded and gestured to Billy; she knew that much.

"Well, the returning soldiers offered to work for the city

for free. Two thousand men, they offered. But they hired Specials instead, for six dollars a day — more than the regular police get paid! They're throwing away money while the people starve. It's outrageous. You be careful out there today with the paper. We don't know who these Specials are, or what they've been told to do."

Billy's face had been turning redder throughout this exchange, and as they emerged onto the street again, he said to Cassie, "Let me sell for you today. Look, it's a lovely day, and I have nothing else to do."

Cassie narrowed her eyes.

"All right. I want to get the measure of these Specials before you're on the street alone all day."

Cassie began to protest, but Mary cut in.

"Cassie, take the day. I'm going to tell Mama I'm taking the day too."

"But you've been more fired up than any of us!" Cassie said.

"It's not about the work," said Mary. "I have an idea."

"It's settled, then," Billy said.

Though she balked at being treated like a child, Cassie had to admit that the Specials looked intimidating. She spotted two as they approached Portage and Main. They were armed with what Billy wryly called "emblems of democracy" — horse's neck yokes sawn in two, about the size of baseball bats. They wore white armbands, a far cry from the smart uniforms the regular police officers wore.

Cassie urged Billy not to bother Freddy, and Billy reluctantly agreed to set up where Cassie did, at a respectful distance. As Billy set up his papers and rock, Mary ran into the café and emerged again after a few minutes.

"Good morning, Red Mary," called Freddy when he saw her.

Mary stalked over to him and Cassie followed worriedly behind. "Do you see what's happened?" Mary hissed in Freddy's face. "The police, who once worked *for* the people, are gone. Now these Specials have come in, with no code of conduct, and we don't know who they are. Do you know what Mrs. Armstrong just told me? Eaton's has supplied these fake officers with horses. Eaton's! Every single person with money in this city is trying to starve us out. And *you're* helping them. You *fool.*"

She stalked away, and Cassie was left scrambling to catch up once again. She turned and waved goodbye to Freddy, who was nonchalantly pulling a cigarette out of his pocket. If she hadn't seen his hand shaking as he brought it up to his mouth, she wouldn't have known how worried he was.

"I truly don't know why you're so friendly with him," Mary was saying. "We don't have time to waste on people who'll never change their minds. We're sacrificing everything to fight this. My mother ..."

"I can imagine," said Cassie quietly. "It's in my house, too. The food, I mean. That's what you were going to say?"

"Yes. The food." Mary slowed her pace. "The café is wonderful, but one meal a day ... we're doing so much better than we were, truly, but I'm so sick of being hungry."

"We have good stores of oatmeal. You could take some home."

Mary rolled her eyes. "Can you imagine what my proud mother would say? Thanks, but I am not ready for that lecture."

Cassie didn't bother mentioning how much Mary had learned about lecturing, judging from her talk with Freddy.

"No, I have another idea," continued Mary. "We need to go by your house first."

Mystified, Cassie walked back to her house.

"You can just wait here," Mary said as she darted through the back door. She came out again quickly, carrying Billy's fishing rod and straw basket that he kept by the door.

She really was a very clever best friend.

Eventually the girls were walking south across Portage to the Assiniboine River. They wandered down Kennedy Street beside the new and magnificent Legislative Building, where the provincial government would soon have its home. The Legislative Building was to have a beautiful impressive dome on top and many beautiful statues. But the dome wasn't finished yet, and there was a fence all around the building's grounds. Cassie stuck her nose through a crack in the fence to get a closer look at the building. She saw men who looked like soldiers putting up tents on the grounds.

"Mary, look!"

"What are they doing?" Mary said, peering through the same crack. "Are they camping out on the grounds? What on earth for?

"I guess it's good weather for camping?" Cassie said as they walked down to the riverbank.

"I don't like it," said Mary. "But I can't figure out exactly why."

Down on the bank, both upstream and down, there were lines stretching into the water all along the banks, although the fishermen were hidden in the Manitoba maple trees. Just another sign of a starving city.

They walked along the river until they found a spot near the bridge. Cassie dug a worm up and put it on the hook, then cast into the shallow brown water.

"I hope I get a pickerel," she said. "Mum cooks it so well." Her stomach growled, and as if in response, Mary's did too. Cassie silently told her stomach to be patient, that there were more important things than food.

"I hope you get twenty pickerels," Mary said, and when Cassie sized up the basket skeptically, Mary responded, "I'll carry them in my arms if I have to!"

The girls turned their faces up to the warm sun and chatted quietly, but there was an ease missing. They needed a catch today.

Eventually, they dozed off in the sunshine, both unused to the long hours they'd been working. After a long nap, Cassie felt the end of her line tug.

"I've got something!" she said. Mary sat up and watched as Cassie reeled in her catch.

When it came to shore, though, Cassie gagged. It wasn't a pickerel or even a whitefish — it was a hideous black fish that looked like an eel. A maria. She took it off the hook and pulled her arm back to throw the disgusting-looking fish back.

"What are you doing?" Mary cried. "Put that down!"

The fish was flopping and twisting in Cassie's hand. "Down? You want to keep it?" she said.

"Put it down," Mary repeated, lifting the rock from the basket. Cassie obeyed, and Mary swiftly killed the fish with the rock. Cassie closed her eyes tight.

"You really aren't used to being hungry, are you?" Mary said as she put the fish into the basket. "Marias are fine to eat. You just have to get past how they look."

Cassie was skeptical, and hooked another worm and cast once more into the water.

"I've never tried them. Can't get past their faces."

"Well, that one doesn't have a face anymore," said Mary cheerfully. "Here, let me hold the rod."

It was a few hours before they had another catch. Mary was pulling in another maria and knocking its head in. Between the heat, her hunger, and the hideous fish, Cassie was beginning to feel woozy.

"Let's pack it in for today," she said. "It must be close to suppertime by now."

"All right," said Mary. "But look around the river. I haven't seen anyone else get a catch. I know you don't feel it, but we got lucky."

"We'll see what Mum can do with it," Cassie sighed, not feeling lucky in the least.

On the way home, Cassie stuck her nose through the fence and watched the soldiers at work again.

"They look ... I don't know, official," she said. "Like they mean business."

"But what business?" said Mary. "And why are they setting up here?"

But Cassie had no answer.

When she got home, she pulled the first maria out of the basket so that Mary could carry hers home out of the heat, said goodbye to her friend, and went inside with the fish and the rod. She found her family sitting around the kitchen table with solemn looks on their faces, holding hot mugs of tea, oatmeal cooking on the stove. Billy's suit jacket was dusty, and his jaunty boater, which he had pulled down off the shelf because of the balmy weather, was on the table in front of him. His tie was all askew. His normally rosy cheeks were extra red, and his eyes were extra blue. It was funny to see him in ordinary clothes.

"And here's Cassie back. Out fishing all day, were you?" said Billy with false heartiness. Everybody looked so worried. Cassie couldn't get over it. What had happened to all their happiness? "Get anything for us?"

"Well ..." said Cassie, wondering if she'd made a mistake bringing the maria home. They might be insulted, thinking it had come to eating something that ugly. But what else could she do? She held up the slippery body of the maria for everyone to see.

"Heavenly days!" shrieked Mrs. Hopkins, clutching her bosom. "What on earth is that? Take it away quickly!" She pointed toward the kitchen sink with one hand, and covered her eyes with the other.

"It's only a maria. It won't hurt. It's dead."

"Dead, she says!" exclaimed Mrs. Hopkins. "Dead!"

"Sorry I couldn't get any pickerel or whitefish. These make good eating too, though. At least, that's what Mary says. I've never —"

"How in heaven's name do I clean a fish like that?" said Mrs. Hopkins. "If it *is* a fish. It looks more like a snake. How will I stand looking at it while I ..." She swallowed bravely and forced a smile at Cassie. "Thank you, Cassie dear. I'm sure it will be just delicious if Mary says so. And it was clever of you girls to go fishing."

Everybody was silent again and stared into space. Cassie gently put her maria in the sink and let the water run over it. For a moment the running water was the only sound.

"I could go out into the country and snare a rabbit," Billy finally suggested. "They're very tasty."

Cassie remembered a dear little brown rabbit she had seen hopping down the lane last fall. Rabbits were so sweet.

"I won't eat a rabbit," she said firmly.

More silence.

"We could always creep up on Mrs. Watson's tomcat," said Billy. Nobody laughed. *Was* it actually possible? thought Cassie. Could they eat Rodney? He was at least fifteen years old, fat and stiff, with chewed-off ears and a scarred old face. Surely Rodney would taste awful, even if he was fat.

"I was joking!" said Billy. "We can't eat Rodney. He's Mrs. Watson's friend. And, you know, a cat. I've heard people talking about poaching deer out in the bush near Charleswood. A buck would do us and the neighbours fine. I'd have to walk out to Charleswood with the rifle, though. I just don't know how long this is going to go on. After what I saw today, it looks as if the police lockout has changed the situation for the worse."

"What did I miss?" said Cassie. One day away from her corner, and there were some important developments to catch up on.

"The streets were full of people — you know what a beautiful day it was. Now, when I direct traffic at the corner of Portage and Main, everything runs smoothly. But just after you left today, things became completely chaotic. Those two Specials were trying to do my job, and they were in a terrible muddle. One was making the traffic go forward while the other was trying to get it to stop. Pretty soon traffic was jammed and people were overflowing the sidewalks into the street."

Cassie giggled. It sounded ridiculous and it served the Specials right.

Billy shook his head as though he wanted her to stop laughing. "The people on foot, mostly strikers, started to tease the two Specials. They yelled, 'Are you afraid of being run over? Are you lost? Does your mother know where you are?' The crowd was having a good holiday time and then along came groups of Specials on foot swinging their clubs, and a woman was struck."

Mrs. Hopkins gasped.

Billy nodded. "It got worse. Along came some Specials on Eaton's ponies and they charged into the crowds of women and children, and the strikers started throwing bottles and bricks, anything. It was around Dingwall's."

"Well, so they should! Riding horses into a crowd of people, that's terrible. Good for the strikers," said Cassie.

"No, bad for the strikers, for all of us. It's terrible. It's exactly what the Citizens' Committee wanted to happen, so they can call in the Mounties and use guns. I think it's a turning point." Billy sighed and glanced over at the sink with the maria in it. "Anyway, I'm off duty until further notice. I think I can get my hands on a car through my friend Daniel's father and use it as a jitney, and give people rides for a nickel, since there are no streetcars. I could use it to drive out and get us a deer or a rabbit. I can make enough to pay for the gasoline and use of the car and still have some left over for income too. It'll bring us a little money, anyway."

Mrs. Hopkins looked over to Mr. Hopkins, who was staring into his mug, his tea untouched. "David," she said.

"Yes, luv?" Mr. Hopkins said without energy. Cassie thought he was probably thinking of his future. He might never be a policeman again. And without the work that Cassie knew he loved, what could he do? Run an elevator in a hotel? Work in the kitchen of a restaurant? He wasn't young anymore.

"David, stop being so gloomy," said Mrs. Hopkins firmly. "Summer is here. And you know what that means. We need to plant the rest of our garden. The sooner we get the vegetables in, the sooner we can eat them. It's almost too late now, and all we've got in is the potatoes, beans, and carrots. We have to think of the future."

"Yes, luvvy," said Mr. Hopkins, sipping his tea.

"When you've finished that, you can take off the storm windows and mend the front steps and patch the screen on the back door. And put up some chicken wire for my sweet peas. Cassie, you should stay home from now on. It's too dangerous to be out on the street."

"I'm not staying off the streets! I've got an important job to do. People still need the bulletin."

"I think it's safe enough," advised Billy. "She's got Freddy, and people know her. She's right by you and Mary and Mrs. Smith in the café. As for me and Dad, I think we need to start looking for other work. Actually, I've been thinking I might even look into working with a threshing team when harvest time comes. It's only temporary money, but it would be a job."

Cassie blinked. Was Billy truly considering not being in the police anymore? Why, that was his life! His future! If he couldn't be a policeman, how could he save his money and meet a sweetheart and get married and have a family of his own?

This strike was changing everything. Cassie thought about herself. Boys and girls just four years older than she was were out working. She wanted to keep learning things, as much as this break from school was nice. But if there was no money at home, she might have to work to contribute to the family. She would be like Freddy. Perhaps she could stay in school somehow and learn to be a typewriter girl. She hoped and hoped.

The mood of the city changed. Whereas before it had been lighthearted, a sort of holiday mood, the atmosphere was now tense and forbidding, and the weather, whose warmth had been so welcome after the long winter, began to get too hot and muggy. People were beginning to wish the strike was over. Many families were on the verge of starvation. People had used up their savings, if they had any in the first place.

The people in charge of the strike were getting grimmer, too. Now when Cassie went into the Labour Café, she would often see Mrs. Armstrong in the corner at a table, writing and writing and not even looking up to greet people or smile at them. She was writing letters to politicians, articles for newspapers across the country, and notes for her many speeches.

Cassie, Mary, and Billy went again to hear J.S. Woodsworth speak at the Labour Church in Victoria Park — which the strikers were calling Liberty Park — and somehow people dug into their pockets and donated a thousand dollars to keep supporting the strikers. Spirits were still high, but Cassie sensed that people were less hopeful. There was less exhilaration and more people looking resigned. A woman standing next to them fainted from standing in the heat for so long, falling heavily against Mary on her way to the ground. Mary stumbled and Billy quickly caught the two and laid the woman down gently while Mary ran to get some water. As Cassie watched her go, she saw several other women swooning. Was it the heat, or was it hunger weakening these women?

* * *

On June 17, about a week after Cassie had caught the maria, she woke with a gnawing hunger. Rather than lying around waiting to feel better, she got up before her father and brother and headed to the Labour Temple a bit earlier than usual to get her papers. Her mother, Mrs. Smith, and Mary had gone to the café earlier today as well, as it was their turn to make the bread. The streets were empty, she assumed because of the early hour.

As she strode toward the doors, her toes hit something and she stumbled. She looked down to see what she'd tripped on and saw the bundled bulletins. Why were they outside? She glanced up and felt a wave of confusion and then a jolt of terror. There was a cordon around the entryway, and the glass of the doors had been shattered. Jagged glass framed the darkened interior of the Temple. Where was everyone? She saw someone moving inside and peered in. When she saw the red of the Mounted Police uniform, she turned on her heel, grabbed her stack of papers, and ran, panicked, to the corner of Portage and Main. As she approached, she heard Freddy shouting, "READ ALL ABOUT IT! MOUNTIES GET THEIR MEN! Strike leaders arrested in dead of night! Taken to Stony Mountain Penitentiary! Read all about it!"

She gasped, dropped the rock on her papers, and bolted toward the Labour Café, nearly running over Mary, who was on her way out.

"Is it true?" asked Cassie. "Tell me it isn't."

"Oh, it's true," said Mary. "I just found out. Mrs. Armstrong isn't coming in today because she and her children are so upset."

Cassie quickly told Mary about the state of the Labour Temple as the two rushed to Cassie's pile of bulletins for more details. Mary quickly skimmed for information. "It says Mounties broke into houses — houses where children were sleeping, mind — turned over their mattresses and bedclothes, held guns to the men's heads, and handcuffed them and took them away to the Stony Mountain Penitentiary. The federal penitentiary! Those walls are twenty feet high, and guards with rifles keep watch in towers. They're treating them like they're dangerous criminals instead of thoughtful leaders."

"It was a Mountie I saw inside the Labour Temple! How could they do this? Do you know who they got other than Mr. Armstrong?"

"No," said Mary. "The bulletin has a list of missing men, but they don't know for certain who was arrested." Her gaze drifted over to Freddy, still hawking the paper as loudly as he could. Her gaze hardened. "I guess there's one way to find out."

She strode over to him. "Freddy," she said.

He straightened. "What is it, Red Mary?"

"Stop it, you two," said Cassie. "Freddy, does your paper list all the men who were taken last night?"

"Oh, so your little bulletin doesn't tell you everything! You need the real newsmen to help you?"

"Who did they get?" Cassie asked frantically.

Mary scanned the page. "My goodness. Five hundred Specials. They sent *five hundred Specials* and fifty Mounties out in the middle of the night. What are they thinking? They can't do this, can they?"

"Mary!" said Cassie. "The names!"

"Yes, they're here. Reverend William Ivens, Russell, Queen, Heaps, Armstrong, Almazoff, Bray, Verenchuk, Choppelrei, and Charitonoff."

"Charitonoff! He's a friend of my father's!" Freddy's mouth fell open and he looked at Cassie.

"So your father's not a traitor like you?" said Mary.

Cassie ignored them. "I guess they haven't got Woodsworth yet," she said grimly. She was beginning to know the score. She looked at the bulletin again and read aloud, her horror deepening. Apparently, Mr. Andrews, the man at the head of the Citizens' Committee of One Thousand, said the arrested strike leaders would be sent home to Britain within seventy-two hours. A law had been passed in Ottawa in just forty minutes saying that the strike leaders could be deported back to Britain. They passed it in order to get the loan from Wall Street. Mr. Andrews would not give the leaders bail; he would not let them pay money in order to stay out of jail. The Immigration Board was coming from Ottawa to deport them all.

At the word "deport," Freddy turned pale alongside Cassie. They both had everything to lose if their own immigrant parents got caught up in everything. Cassie was especially worried about passionate, furious Billy doing something to get himself deported.

"You're not getting deported," Mary said to Cassie. "I won't let them do it. Let me see that."

She took the bulletin back from Cassie's limp hand and said, "Here, now, you didn't tell me this. People in twenty cities in North America have stopped working because *we've* stopped working! Even people in England are supporting the strike. This is bigger than us," she said, a bit breathless. "This is bigger than we ever imagined. We're doing it!" She shot a triumphant look at Freddy.

"But why did they throw everybody in jail?" Cassie said, unable to move on.

"They want to scare people, that's all." Freddy sat down on the sidewalk and pulled some tobacco and some papers out of his pocket and began rolling himself a cigarette.

"Can they really send people back to England?"

"They can do anything they want." Freddy shrugged, struggling to look like he didn't care. Strands of tobacco peeked out from each end of the cigarette paper as he rolled it into a tube.

"I need to get back to the café," said Mary. "Come see me if you hear anything else, and I'll do the same."

Cassie nodded and watched as Mary glanced contemptuously at Freddy and strode back to the café.

CHAPTER 8

Cassie found Billy weeding the small potato mounds in the back garden when she got home after selling out the bulletin. Her customers had been quiet and sombre today.

"What will we do with the strike leaders in jail? How will we organize the bulletin?" she asked immediately.

"Well, hello to you too, dear sister. You heard, did you? I suppose a papergirl never misses the news." Billy's words were playful, but his eyes were so worried.

"What will we even do with the paper without the strike leaders to make it?"

"Don't worry about the bulletin; Woodsworth is taking over. That's how they got the bulletin out at all today, with news of the arrests. He'll do a fine job. You just keep pounding the pavement and letting the good folk know what's happening. I'm proud of the work you're doing. I know it hasn't turned out as fun as you thought it might."

Cassie looked at her brother, so recently a fine police

officer, pulling weeds out of the earth. He looked scraggly. "I don't think anyone's having as much fun as they thought."

Billy laughed. "Well, to be fair, Cassie, none of the grownups were really in this for the fun. Here, let's go in. I've got supper cooking."

"Good. Mum has enough to do at the café all day without having to cook for you layabouts."

"Ouch," said her brother as he opened the back door.

Expecting the smell of oatmeal, starchy and bland, to hit her, Cassie opened the door to the mouthwatering aroma of stewed meat. It had been weeks since she'd caught the whiff of anything so delicious.

"What did you do? Are we about to eat the cat?" she said eagerly as she rushed to the table.

Her father appeared from the parlour. "Let's not ask any questions, luv," he said. "Let's just enjoy it."

Cassie stopped in her tracks. "I was *joking*. What is it?" She ran to the front window to see if she could spy fat Rodney in Mrs. Watson's front garden. There he was, fur gleaming as he lay in the sun. "Okay, not Rodney. So what, then?"

Billy just shook his head sternly at her, and the scent of the meat, with its promise of a calm, full stomach, brought her to her chair as Billy filled the bowls.

When Mrs. Hopkins came through the back door a few minutes later, supper was on the table and her family was waiting eagerly for her arrival.

"Not a word, Mum," said Billy when he saw her open her mouth. "Not about the food, not about the strike, not about the arrests, not about deportation — not about anything. Just sit. Eat."

The family sat in silence, reverent before the rich stew in front of them.

"Billy, is this —" Cassie began.

"Shh. Eat."

She resisted for a moment, suspicious of this meat's provenance, but her body took over and made the decision for her. Though the stew had very little in the way of vegetables, Billy had scrounged an onion and a couple of old carrots from somewhere. The meat was delicate and tender, rich and nourishing. The broth was salty and little droplets of fat shone in the liquid. Though the day was still hot, Cassie was not bothered by the warmth of the stew. She felt it travelling down to the tips of her toes and she welcomed its heat.

She tried to savour the meal, but she finished her entire bowl in fewer than five minutes. When she looked up, she realized her family had done the same. As one, they sat back in their chairs and sighed.

"You've outdone yourself, son. Thank you. I'm sorry our food's been so scarce."

Billy looked at his mother. "It's scarce for everyone, except the bosses. You know that. You and Dad have done your best, but I thought we could all use a little boost." He saw Cassie start to speak again and said, "Cassie, if you keep asking questions, you'll get answers you don't like. But tonight you'll be going to bed with a full belly and enough strength to keep working tomorrow."

Cassie tried to protest, but her body felt so full and happy that she couldn't. She pushed away the thought of fuzzy little rabbits, cleared the table, washed the dishes, and went straight to bed.

CHAPTER 9

On her way to the Labour Temple to get the papers the next morning, her body still humming happily from the stew the night before, Cassie chatted with Mary. Their mothers were walking a little behind them. They didn't always accompany the girls as far as the Labour Temple, but the morning was fine and clear and they were happy to have an extra bit of fresh air before spending the day in the hot kitchen.

When they reached the Temple, they were surprised to find Mrs. Armstrong waiting outside in front of the patched doors. She was standing among a small crowd of about seven children, many whom Cassie recognized from Carlton School's poor families. She gave them a big smile. She'd missed some of her classmates and fellow baseball players. Before she had a chance to say hello, Mrs. Armstrong was speaking.

"Oh good!" she said. "I was hoping to catch my favourite kitchen helper and papergirl. And your mothers are here too; excellent. Ladies, we have an important mission for which you and your daughters are needed."

Cassie could see her mother and Mrs. Smith stand a little straighter.

"What is it?" said Mrs. Smith. "Is the kitchen okay?"

"It's more than okay, with you two working in it. Today, I need you both to run the kitchen, in fact. Anna, I'd like you to manage the volunteers. Ruth, you'll be in charge of the food. I know you'll do an excellent job. You've already saved me the trouble of going over there."

Mrs. Hopkins managed to swallow her shock enough to ask, "But where will you be? Are you all right? Is it George? What's ..." She gestured to the children around Mrs. Armstrong. "What's all this?"

"I'm fine, and George is all right for now, although he's in prison, as I know you've heard. So, I'm bringing some children to the penitentiary. I want to show the government how ridiculous it is to have those men in a federal penitentiary. They're not dangerous revolutionaries or aliens; they're hard workers looking for a better deal for all of us. I'm taking some strikers' children to sing outside the walls."

Just then a truck drew up, its large covered bed surrounded with chicken wire.

"Which brings me to you two," said Mrs. Armstrong. "Will you join us? If your mothers say it's all right, that is."

"What about my corner?" said Cassie.

"I've got a young man inside who said he'll fill in today — one of your brother's policeman friends who's at a loose end now. What do you say?"

Mary couldn't help but give a little hop. "Yes!" she said. "I'm coming! Mother, I can, can't I?"

It was a testament to how much trust Mrs. Smith had in Mrs. Armstrong that she didn't even hesitate. "Of course, dear."

Before Cassie could ask, her mother said, "Yes, yes, Cassie. You mind your manners and do what Mrs. Armstrong tells you to." She gave Cassie a quick kiss and a hug.

"I don't want to rush you, but it's about eleven miles out to the penitentiary, so we had better get a move on if we want to be back in time for lunch."

Cassie and Mary piled into the truck along with the other children. Mrs. Armstrong sat up at the front with the driver.

The truck rumbled away from the Temple and through the streets, along Elgin to Isabel and eventually over the Salter Street Bridge. It was strange to see the warehouses shuttered as they passed through the city, with people out on the streets instead of at work. Few trains were on the tracks. The city was far from quiet, but it was a different kind of busy from usual. As they drove along McPhillips out of the city, Mary saw the buildings trickle to just occasional barns and farmhouses.

Soon Mrs. Armstrong climbed back with them and began teaching them a song called "Solidarity Forever." Cassie had heard it a few times at the Labour Church but hadn't learned all the words. It was a song written a few years earlier by an American during a coal miners' strike.

"Can anyone tell me what solidarity is?" asked Mrs.

Armstrong after she'd told them the words to the song.

One boy, Mark, from the grade below Cassie and Mary at Carlton School, raised his hand. "When something's really solid, like a rock?"

Cassie snorted and Mary elbowed her hard. "Be nice," she hissed.

"Hm, not quite," said Mrs. Armstrong, much more patiently than Cassie could have. "Solidarity is working together, having a common cause. It's what this whole strike is built out of. Without solidarity, there'd be no unions. Let's try the song together now, and let's really think about what solidarity is."

Cassie, Mary and the other children sang the song until they had all the words memorized, as the truck rolled down country roads and through beautiful fields of green. It was hot, still, but the country held cool breezes and sweet smells — except when they were passing too close to pigs — and Cassie felt her worried spirits lift. By the time the truck pulled up to the Stony Mountain Penitentiary, the children knew the song forwards and backwards.

The penitentiary was just as described: twenty-foot-tall stone walls, with guard towers looming ominously over the children.

"All right, everyone!" said Mrs. Armstrong. "We're going to walk over to the gates to sing. Follow me."

She hopped down from the truck and the children began to jump down after her, walking slowly toward the prison, which looked enormous next to them. Cassie could see movement in the guard towers, and she knew that's where the guards were holding guns. More guards stood by the gates, looking stern and mean.

Cassie leaned over to Mary. "I don't feel so well. I think I'll just stay in the truck."

Mary looked a bit grey herself, but she grabbed Cassie's hand. "Think of the men inside there, and how they must feel," she said. "Maybe they'll hear us — think of that. We could bring them some comfort."

"You're right. I know that."

"Come on then, silly."

Reluctantly, Cassie stood and jumped down behind Mary, and they quickly caught up with the rest of the group.

"Everybody all right?" said Mrs. Armstrong, smiling a bit sadly at Cassie.

"Yes, we're fine." What was Cassie thinking? Mrs. Armstrong had had men in her house taking her husband away in the middle of the night, and now she was here. If she could be so brave, Cassie could certainly sing this song.

The group gathered by the gates, so close they could see the triggers on the guards' rifles.

"You can't come in with those children," shouted one man.

"Not planning to, thank you," said Mrs. Armstrong curtly. Turning to the children, she hummed a note, then counted, "One, two, three." They sang the first verse:

When the union's inspiration through the workers'
blood shall run,

> *There can be no power greater anywhere beneath the*
> *sun.*
> *Yet what force on earth is weaker than the feeble*
> *strength of one,*
> *But the union makes us strong.*

As they sang the words together, Cassie closed her eyes. She was swept up in a feeling. It was the same feeling she'd had an echo of at Labour Church, or sometimes when there were dozens of people clamouring for the bulletin. This time, though, it was much stronger. A feeling of power, but a different sort of power than the one held over the strikers by the mayor and the Mounties and the Specials. This power came from the ground and travelled up through her belly, and she felt like she shared it with every other worker there was. She felt the power spinning out of her mouth with the song, her voice joining the others' voices, like they were vines climbing up and over the stone walls of the penitentiary. The vines grew between the cracks of the stones, sending shoots into the cells beyond. In Cassie's mind, the vines of the children's song were strong enough to tear down the whole prison and set everyone free.

As the final verse started, Cassie was surprised to feel tears streaming down her cheeks. Still she kept her eyes closed.

> *In our hands is placed a power greater than their*
> *hoarded gold,*
> *Greater than the might of armies, multiplied a*
> *thousand-fold.*

We can bring to birth a new world from the ashes of
the old
For the union makes us strong.

Solidarity forever
Solidarity forever
Solidarity forever
The union makes us strong.

When the song ended, Mrs. Armstrong said, "Again, children." They started the song at the beginning. Cassie opened her eyes to find the prison still standing, the guards still frowning, but nevertheless there was something different. She was connected now to her friends and classmates, to Mrs. Armstrong, to every worker starving in order to make things more fair. Mark hadn't been entirely wrong then; solidarity *was* very solid, like a rock. She could feel it.

After an hour of singing, the children were tired and thirsty, their voices beginning to rasp. "Back into the truck, everyone," said Mrs. Armstrong, and she handed out cookies and passed around a big jar of water.

Some of the children played clapping games on the ride back, but Cassie and Mary held hands and looked out at the fields. Cassie wondered if Mary had had the same feelings of the power in their song, of solidarity.

Then she heard Mary humming the chorus to their song under her breath, and Cassie decided that was all the answer she needed.

CHAPTER 10

B ack on her corner the next day, Cassie saw Freddy.
"Did you miss me, Freddy?"

He just grunted.

"Don't you want to know where I was yesterday?"

"Not especially."

"I went to jail, that's where."

He looked up sharply at that, searching her face. "That a joke?"

"No, I really was there. Just to sing, though. With Mrs. Armstrong. For all those men in jail, you know? Your father's friend?"

He looked away again. "Mm."

"Are you okay, Freddy? You don't seem like yourself."

"Myself? How would you know what that is?" he said.

Cassie felt hurt; she thought they'd become friends. "Sorry," she said. "You seem a bit sad, that's all."

Freddy looked at the corner, at the Specials guiding traffic where Billy should have been. "The strike is ruining my sales. No one has the money for the paper. I'm not sure

... my family. They're getting hungrier and there's nothing I can do about it." His face clouded. "Everything was *fine* before the strike started. We were doing all right. I can't take much more of this."

Cassie didn't argue with him, but she knew it wasn't true. If everything had been all right before the strike, Freddy would have been in school, not supporting his whole family.

* * *

The next day, Friday, June 20, Cassie entered the kitchen to find Billy at the kitchen table, bleary-eyed, drinking black tea and looking very rumpled.

"What's wrong?" she asked.

Billy's tired eyes twinkled nevertheless above the steaming cup. "Late night," he said.

"Another strike meeting? Any news?"

He looked like he was going to say something, then set his cup down and said, "Tell you what, why don't we walk to the Temple together to get your papers, and you can see for yourself."

"Why the big mystery?" she asked, pulling her shoes on.

They walked the city blocks together, Billy uncharacteristically quiet, but he didn't seem upset. When they finally reached the Temple and Cassie opened the front door to reach for her bundle of papers, she let out a scream. Billy whooped in response.

STRIKE LEADERS OUT, the headline said, in giant bold letters. Cassie skimmed the article. "A dozen cars left the Labour Temple ... a crowd of some forty or fifty people gathered round the main entrance of the penitentiary," she read aloud. "Good grief, Billy. You went out there in the middle of the night?"

Billy grinned. "We got the warden up and made him open the doors. They're allowed out on bail! Andrews is getting burned for it in the big papers. They think he's being too soft on us."

"So they'll be back! Is Mr. Armstrong here?" she said.

Billy sobered a little. "Well, in order to make bail, they had to swear they wouldn't be involved in the strike or the Labour Committee at all anymore. So none of them are allowed near us or this place at all."

"What will we do without our leaders?"

"Oh," said Billy, "haven't you been paying attention? The Citizens' Committee's mistake is thinking they can just arrest a few leaders and make this all go away. They don't realize that the leaders are no different from the rest of us. That's the whole point of a union. They take away the leaders we have, we'll just find new ones, that's all."

Cassie hugged her tired brother — and no wonder he was tired, up all night rescuing strike leaders from prison — and walked to her corner, buoyed by the news.

* * *

A few hours later, Mary came out of the café to tell Cassie what she'd just learned: The returned soldiers had met an hour earlier in Old Market Square and decided to call a silent parade for two thirty the next afternoon — Saturday, June 21. They would march to the Royal Alexandra Hotel to ask Senator Robertson what he'd been doing during the strike. Only the returned soldiers, with their wives and children, would march. The strikers would all watch silently to give their support. Everyone was going, including the Hopkins family and Mary and her mother.

On Saturday morning, however, Billy told Mary that Mayor Gray had issued a proclamation that any women taking part in a parade would do so at their own risk.

"The mayor must think women are weaklings or something," Cassie said to Billy and Mary as the two families walked down Portage Avenue to Main Street to see the parade.

People filled the sidewalks, everyone heading north on Main Street to City Hall.

"I think we should stick together in case anything happens," suggested Billy. "But the crowd is quite calm."

"What time is it, David?" Mrs. Hopkins asked, holding onto her hat with one hand.

Mr. Hopkins pulled his big gold pocket watch from his vest and flicked it open. "Just two thirty now," he said, snapping the watch shut.

Billy strained to look over the crowd. "I can see the soldiers assembling ahead. They've got their wives and children with them."

Cassie saw Mary and her mother exchange a quick look, clearly remembering the soldier missing from their own family. Mary took her mother's hand and they both looked back to the crowds, trying in vain to see overtop all the other onlookers.

A man in front turned around and said, "The soldier committee is still interviewing Senator Robertson. When they come back the parade will start."

All Cassie could see were backs and legs and straw hats and ears. She hoped Billy would offer to put her on his shoulders.

"You can't see anything from down there," he said as if he could read her mind. "Climb up on my shoulders." So she climbed up on his back and Billy slowly straightened up.

Now she could see everything. In every direction, there were people milling and waiting to take part in a peaceful protest. She couldn't believe the masses of people! More, even, than attended Labour Church.

But the blossoming warmth in her heart was quickly chilled by what she saw. She grabbed Billy's hair and pushed his hat over his eyes.

"Hey! Don't do that!" Billy exclaimed.

"Billy! All these Mounties on horses are riding right towards us, and they've got baseball bats and they're swinging them! They hit someone — and someone else!"

"What?" yelled Billy. "Mounties! Why, those— This is a trap!"

"Some of them are Specials. And I see soldiers. Soldiers on both sides!" She thought back to the encampment she and Mary had seen by the new Legislative Building. That puzzle piece slid into place. Not all the returning soldiers were on the strikers' side. Some were clearly working for the government, against the workers.

"David," said Mrs. Hopkins in a nervous voice, tugging

at his arm. "Let's get over to the sidewalk where it's safe."

"Us too, Mama," said Mary.

"Yes," said Mrs. Smith. "I'd rather not be caught up in this." They hastily retreated and disappeared, swallowed by the hordes.

"The crowd is opening up and letting the horses through," Cassie reported. "Now the street is full of people again." All around them, they could hear angry hisses and boos, and people were picking up rocks from a building site and throwing them at the Mounties and the other men with them.

"Booooo!" jeered the people, and rocks flew through the air. Cassie saw two horses without riders galloping down Main Street. She was clinging to Billy's hair with one hand, and he was holding her by the leg and trying to hold on to his hat.

Squirming around, Cassie saw her mother disappearing to the safety of the City Hall grounds, with her father limping along behind. He turned and motioned with his hand for Billy and Cassie to follow.

But the Mounties were swinging around again. This time they had drawn their revolvers, which glinted menacingly in the sunshine. Cassie was aware, suddenly, of how high her head was sticking above the crowd.

"Billy! Let me down! They have their revolvers!" The Mounties were charging straight into the crowd across the street, firing their revolvers. Bang! Bang! The guns cracked into the air, and people scrambled and stumbled over one another to get out of the way. Screams tore through the air as Cassie fell from Billy's shoulders. She clutched at his trouser leg with both hands as he was trying to run, and then he took her wrist and they were pushed along with the crowd as it rushed away from the guns.

As they ran towards the Union Bank, Cassie felt her foot brush against something soft and just avoided tripping. She looked down and saw a person — an old man. There was blood running down his face and his eyes stared straight up into the sky. Cassie covered her mouth with her hand, trying not to be sick. This man was dead. The bullets were real. One might hit her or Billy, might hit their parents or Mary or Mrs. Smith or any of the innocent people who had come here to protest today. Billy pulled on her wrist till it hurt, but a big man blocked her way and pushed Billy ahead of him and his grip on her wrist soon hurt so much that her hand was turning blue. His hand finally slid away and disappeared between bodies and legs. Cassie stumbled at the curb, afraid of falling and being trampled by the running people and never getting up again. Her heart beat very fast, and she felt that her body would fall apart before she got somewhere safe. She wondered if she would survive.

The Mounties were firing at people's legs as they ran. There was more space now, and she stopped to catch her breath. She saw the Mounties riding back, twirling their smoking revolvers in the air like cowboys.

Then Cassie heard a great noise nearby. Volunteers — scabs — had been running the streetcars to make the strikers mad, and it looked like a striker had pulled the trolley off. A crowd of men were trying to push the streetcar over.

Some boys were ripping off a piece of the streetcar and left it lying in the street. Then the seats were on fire and Cassie could smell smoke. The burning streetcar swayed and toppled above the heads of the crowd.

Cassie was panting, trying to catch her breath, as she looked desperately around for Billy or her parents, or even the useless Freddy. Her hair was falling in her eyes, and her face was smudged with dirt and tears. Suddenly she felt an arm around her shoulders. Gasping, she turned, ready to fight off the Mountie holding on to her, but to her relief it was Mary.

"Where's your mother?" she asked quickly.

Mary shook her head. "We got separated. I can't believe I found you. What about your family?"

"Separated. I saw a dead body. People are *dying*. We need to get out of here. Come on." She grabbed Mary's hand and ran towards City Hall, the last place she'd seen her parents. In the distance, she could see lines of Specials forming across Main Street, swinging big clubs. The Mounties had gotten off their horses and were lined up across the street. Mary pulled her and they ran behind the City Hall to Old Market Square.

The girls stopped in their tracks and gasped. Soldiers in armoured cars with big guns mounted in the back were driving up and down the street.

"The city must be under military control," Mary said. "Ma Armstrong worried this would happen."

"Do you think the soldiers really mean to use those guns on us?" Cassie was quaking down to her toes.

"The Mounties already have," said Mary. "But they're not shooting right now. We need to get back to your house before things get worse. Maybe we can make it. Come on."

"But our parents, and Billy —"

"Would correctly point out that we're just children and we do not belong here. We need to go *now*."

They slipped off down a side street, then broke into a run, still gripping each other's hands. Cassie pulled them into a lane to get away from the fray but saw a man with a dirty white armband on his sleeve, the sign of the Specials, lying on his back. Another man was straddling him, punching him again and again in the face. It must have been a striker. Weren't they supposed to be protesting peacefully? But then, it was the Mounties and the Specials who had changed that.

Cassie could feel Mary pulling toward the men, as though she could stop this. Cassie yanked her firmly back, and Mary seemed to come to her senses. They turned and started to run again, and Cassie could hear footsteps coming behind her, getting closer and closer, until a man passed her, running full tilt away from a Special brandishing a club. Nearby, a riderless horse was tripping over its reins and whinnying. On a street corner, Cassie saw a Mountie holding a gun pointed toward the crowds rushing by. She yanked Mary along even faster.

"Did you see?" she said breathlessly.

"Yes. Keep going," said Mary.

Cassie could barely believe what was happening in her city. The Mounties were meant to be noble protectors of the people. But they were just working for the rich bosses, threatening and killing — actually killing — peaceful protestors.

The girls raced down Princess Street, past all the warehouses and clothing factories and fur traders. Cassie dodged down a shortcut through the space between two of the buildings and pulled Mary down a narrow alleyway. But the passage ended in a tiny opening strewn with broken glass and closed in by a jagged, unpainted fence. Mary and Cassie looked at each other. Then before Cassie knew it, Mary was over the fence. Cassie heard her yell and scrambled up behind her friend. Once at the top of the fence, she paused a moment to heave her legs up behind her. There below her was a group of boys standing around someone lying bleeding on the ground, Mary looking on in horror. The boys looked up in surprise to see her. It was Nick the Stick and his friends. And the boy they were beating up was Freddy!

"The Bolshie!" cried one boy. "And the papergirl!"

"They're both Reds," said Nick the Stick. "Don't let them get away!"

"Freddy!" screamed Cassie, pausing long enough at the top of the fence to make sure it was her friend. Freddy didn't respond. But it was soon clear that the boys were turning their attention away from the bloodied boy and toward her, and she dropped down to the ground and turned to run back in the direction she'd come from. As she fell, she saw Mary dropping to the ground to help Freddy. Good. The boys would stay away from her friends if they were chasing her. The boys pushed a loose board in the fence and squeezed through one by one, then picked up speed as they followed Cassie between the brick walls.

They hollered and hooted like a hockey team on the move. "Let's get her! We'll show her who runs this town now!"

Cassie headed back to City Hall, where she hoped there would be more people who could intervene. The boys were picking up rocks as they ran and were throwing them at Cassie, roaring as they charged.

"Hey, Red! Red!" She could hear Nick the Stick's voice closing in behind her. "Slow down a minute, Red!" Cassie wondered who could help her now that the city was under military control. She couldn't ask the Specials; they were on the side of these hooligans. And so were the Mounties.

She had never been so terrified in her life.

Suddenly something heavy hit her on the back of the head, and her knees went wobbly. She fell face first with the force of the blow. Everything went black.

CHAPTER 11

The next thing Cassie knew, somebody was turning her over gently. She tried to open her eyes, but the light was too bright, and she closed them tightly again. Her head hurt all over. She kept her eyes closed as someone's hand pressed her back and helped her sit up, very slowly. She tried to resist in case it was Nick and his friends, but the world whirled around her. She reached up and felt the back of her head with her hand. Through her tangled hair, she could distinguish a large lump. When she took her hand away, she finally opened her eyes to look at her fingers. They were red with blood. The sight of it made her feel as if her stomach had come loose and was floating about inside of her. Then she noticed out the corner of her eye the ring of legs around the spot where she sat on the ground. Somebody was crouching down close to her with an arm around her shoulders, and a hand smoothed the hair away from her face.

"Cass?"

She looked up. Billy!

"You okay, Cass?"

"Oh, Billy!" cried Cassie, throwing her arms around his neck and then regretting the sudden movement as her stomach lurched. "How did you find me?"

"You ran right into me. My friends and I were searching down the back alleys stopping fights when you came around the corner with a screaming pack of young hoodlums in hot pursuit. As soon as they saw us, they turned and ran, but we managed to catch this one. He's the biggest, but he can't run very fast. Bertie here brought him down like a ton of bricks."

Cassie's blurred vision slowly focused on the notorious Nick the Stick, who was being held up by the collar of his jacket like a sack of flour. He looked pretty scared. All the bravado and sneering confidence he had with his gang had drained right out of him.

Then Cassie remembered.

"Freddy!" she cried. "They were beating him up. I saw him lying on the ground. They were kicking him and punching him. Eight of them. Mary's with him." She saw movement beyond the circle around her and squinted. "There they are!"

Cassie pointed at a forlorn pair approaching the gathering. Freddy was limping, his shirt was torn and bloody, and he was holding his ribs and scowling. He was leaning heavily on Mary, whose arm was around his waist. But at least he was walking. People parted and let them into the centre of the ring.

Cassie stood gingerly and staggered over to them, dizzy

and sick. She hugged both her friends. "Freddy!" she said. "I thought you were done for!"

"Nah," said Freddy, wincing a bit. "I'll live. I'm pretty good with my fists, y'know. I can usually take care of myself. But eight against one … I'm not sure what I would've done if you hadn't come along and distracted them. And Red M — I mean, Mary. She helped me once you all left."

"I was sure he was dead. I'm so sorry I didn't go with you, Cassie. Are you okay? You look terrible."

"Thanks a lot. I think I'll be okay. I'm so glad I got those boys away from you two. But why'd they pick on you, Freddy? They usually leave you alone."

"'Cause when I saw what the Mounties done, and I saw those boys cheering them on, I lost it. I decided I was proud to be a Ukranian, and so I told them. I tried to fight Nick the Stick alone, but the others wouldn't stand for a fair fight, so …"

"Is he the one who hit you with the rock?" one of Billy's mates asked Cassie in a kind voice.

"Lord," sighed Cassie, "I don't know *who* hit me with that rock, but I'll tell you this, Nick definitely owes me four dollars and twenty cents."

"Let me at him," growled Freddy. "I'll bust his nose in." Freddy tried to separate himself from Mary's supporting arm and nearly fell to the ground.

"I don't think you'll be busting any noses in for at least another few minutes," Mary said drily, lowering him gently and sitting beside him.

"Wait a minute," said Billy, squinting at Nick's face.

"This is Nick MacKenzie, isn't it? Son of Clyde MacKenzie, one of the biggest lawyers in town and a ringleader of the Committee of One Thousand? With a daddy as rich as his, I'm sure he's got four dollars and twenty cents to spare for the strike committee. Hey, Richard, turn the kid upside down. See if his pockets are jingling like I think they are."

The man holding Nick dropped him suddenly, then picked him up by the ankles and shook him hard.

"Wait a minute!" squealed Nick. A few pennies fell to the ground and bounced away. "Put me down! Put me down! I'll pay you, you money-grubbing Bolshies." Richard lowered Nick to the ground. Nick stood up, brushed himself off carefully, and dug deep in his pockets. He pulled out a carefully folded five-dollar bill, which he held out to Cassie.

"Just let me punch him in the nose," Freddy growled menacingly again, but if anything, he started leaning more heavily on Mary.

"You might as well take the fiver," said Billy. "Keep the whole thing. I'm sure the MacKenzies can spare the change."

Cassie reached out and took the bill from Nick the Stick, then tucked it into her dress pocket. Her head hurt something awful, but she felt better. Lighter.

Suddenly, it came to her in a flash. She had been paid back. Nick had wronged her and hurt Freddy badly, but things were coming right again. He had been caught, and good people had made him own up, and a knot she hadn't even realized was inside her had come untangled.

Justice. *This* was how it felt. Billy was right. Remarkable.

Nick the Stick turned and pushed his way out through

the ring of people. His cheeks were red and his ears glowed with humiliation. He turned back, his eyes hard as steel, and with a voice full of venom, said, "You'll pay. You'll pay for what you've done. My father will see to it that none of you ever work again! When you're looking for a job, when you're trying to find someplace to live, when you're looking for something to eat, just remember who runs this town. We've put you down once and for all. Don't say we didn't warn you, you disgusting revolutionaries!"

But the gang of people around Cassie ignored him. There were much bigger forces at play than a little bully like Nick the Stick. And anyway, if this was how the Russian rulers had treated the people, they'd been right to have a revolution, and maybe there *was* one needed in Canada too.

"Know what they're calling today?" said Billy solemnly to Cassie, as everyone watched Nick angrily stomp away. "Bloody Saturday. Last count there were more than thirty people wounded by the Mounties."

"Worse than wounded. I saw a dead man. I almost stepped on him." Cassie shuddered at the memory.

Her brother gave her a gentle hug.

"Has anyone seen my mother?" Mary asked softly.

"Haven't caught up with anyone else we know yet," said Billy. "Soon, I hope. The crowds are breaking up. We should get home, maybe see our families there. How's your head now, Cassie?"

"Sore," she admitted. "I'll probably need to lean on you like Freddy needs Mary. Since when will you two even look at each other, anyway, let alone practically cuddle?"

Freddy tried again to stand up without support but still couldn't manage it.

"Oh, stop fussing," said Mary. "I'll take you back to Cassie's and we'll get you a bit of ... well, oatmeal, I suppose. And clean you up before we send you home. But let's hurry. I want to see if my mother was caught in the ..." She trailed off, not sure how to describe the day.

"I guess you could call it a massacre," said Billy. "The Mounties are calling it a riot, of course. Putting the blame on us. Like they didn't ride into the crowd with their clubs swinging and their guns firing, alongside all those Specials. Imagine, policemen behaving that way. But I'm sure all our parents are fine. They got away quickly."

The group began to move slowly toward the Hopkinses' street. Cassie, dizzy and sore, leaned on Billy's arm. She was behind Mary and Freddy, and she could hear Mary talking.

"You know, Freddy, since I have you here ..."

Freddy groaned.

"You should stop sucking up to your bosses. They've shown their true colours, don't you think? Nick knows you work for his father's friends and he had no trouble nearly killing you."

"I wouldn't have let them kill —"

"You know full well they would've kept going if Cassie hadn't distracted them. The only thing they hate more than an alien is a girl who doesn't know her place, and a lucky thing that is for you. You know, you could get the other newsboys together and start a union! Bet you could make more money. You've got some power. They need *someone* to sell their papers for them. And," she said grudgingly, "you do a good job of it, even if the papers are full of lies. They're lucky to have someone like you on the corner. Why don't you make them pay you more, enough that you could feed your family a little better?"

"Nobody's gonna make me do nothin'," said Freddy.

"That's my point. Nobody's making you. It just makes sense, that's all. And once you newsboys are unionized, *you'll* be making the *bosses* do things, do right."

"Oh, I'll think about it. How about that?"

The ragtag group stumbled back to the Hopkinses', where, to the great relief of the children, they found Mr. and Mrs. Hopkins as well as Mary's mother. Mrs. Smith cried out when she saw Mary's clothes covered with blood and was visibly relieved when she realized it had come from Freddy's nose. Freddy clearly tried not to be offended. She swiftly set to tending his wounds while Mrs. Hopkins guided Cassie to the parlour and had her lie down on the Chesterfield.

Cassie had never enjoyed being fussed over so much in her entire life.

CHAPTER 12

Cassie slept heavily that night, and although she was a bit woozy in the morning, she insisted on returning to the street to sell the bulletin.

"I'm only letting you so I can keep you closer to me," said her mother as they walked slowly to Portage and Main. "And I expect you to come in to the café and sit for at least ten minutes every hour."

"Yes, Mum," she said.

"Especially since Freddy won't be back," she said, "and Billy is in more godforsaken meetings all day."

"I thought he said meetings were banned now," Cassie said.

"Yes," said her mother. "No big meetings. Which means no Labour Church, and no raising money to feed all our girls. But they won't find out about Billy's little meetings."

The streets were quiet, as if the whole city were holding an extended moment of silence for the life and liberties lost and the people injured in yesterday's attack on the workers. Cassie was gazing off down the road and remembering the horrors she'd seen the day before when she heard a call behind her: "GET yer PAYper HERE ..."

She turned. He stood there, bruised and a little hunched over as though his stomach hurt, but standing on his own. "Freddy! What on earth are you doing back?"

"Can't stop me from working," he said. "I'll work till I'm dead." Again, the bravado, despite the slight tremble in his voice. He'd been badly hurt the day before. This boy would never admit defeat.

"Well, glad to have you here to protect me," said Cassie, and Freddy couldn't help but grin at that. Then Cassie set to selling the bulletin to the few who wandered by.

When an hour was up, she kept her promise to her mother and went into the café. It was as busy as ever; Cassie supposed even massacres didn't stop people needing food. But the volume of conversation was quieter than usual. Cassie could see Mrs. Armstrong in the kitchen, looking sombre and furious. But she shot a quick smile at Cassie when she came out.

"Your mother tells me you were quite the warrior yesterday, though you should never have had to be. I'm so impressed with you, papergirl."

Cassie reddened, tongue-tied. What could she say to her hero?

Mary emerged from the kitchen carrying a couple of biscuits and two cups of tea.

"Here," she said. "These are for you and for the traitor, too."

"Really?" said Cassie, glancing at Mrs. Armstrong.

"Yes, really," said the older woman. "That boy needs some nourishment if he's going to be strong enough to be worth recruiting." She winked at the girls and settled at a nearby table with a paper and pen. Ready to write to papers across the country, Cassie guessed. Ready to tell everyone what had happened in the streets yesterday. Ready to tell everyone how brave the strikers were in the face of armed bullies and military rule. Ready to *force* everyone to see how wrong the bosses and the government were.

Cassie carried the biscuits and two cups of tea out to Freddy. He eyed them suspiciously.

"Bolshevism isn't contagious, Freddy. The worst you're going to be is disappointed there's no butter."

* * *

Cassie kept working for the next few days, but there were fewer and fewer people buying bulletins.

On Tuesday, June 24, the girls met on Portage and walked together to Main. Cassie waved to Freddy and set up her rock and papers while Mary made her way to the café. But Mary bolted out again a few minutes later, frantic.

"What is it?" Cassie called, racing over.

Mary ran, panting and frantic. "Mrs. Armstrong's gone! She's been put in jail!"

Cassie felt her stomach sink like a rock. It couldn't be! "That's not fair!"

"Apparently they've told the women prisoners that because they're not acting like ladies, they won't be treated like ladies."

Cassie's mouth hardened. "Well, if being treated like a lady means being paid half as much as a man to work in an unsafe factory, then maybe it's for the best," she said.

Mary took a deep breath. "We just have to keep fighting, right? It's what she would do. We have to keep on without her till she's out."

Cassie glanced at the café, catching a glimpse of her mother looking distraught. "Yes. It's what she would do, because it's all any of us *can* do."

* * *

"There's just as many people asking for food," Mary told Cassie on Wednesday evening as they walked home, "but so much less food to prepare. We're having to turn people away with almost nothing in their bellies, now that we can't raise money for the café at Labour Church. My mother — well, you saw her this morning. She's so weak, Cassie. She'll get sick. What am I going to do?"

Mary didn't have to wonder for long. The very next day, on June 26, the strike committee called off the strike.

Even though people were starving, even though they couldn't raise any more money to feed people because meetings had been banned, the strikers didn't want to call it quits. But the strike committee was adamant. The violence on Bloody Saturday had been too much. They needed to stop the strike before something worse happened, before any more people died.

CHAPTER 13

"Hurry, Cassie," said Mary.

Cassie ran out the door, shoes untied.

"How is it that you made it to sell the bulletin on time every single day, but our first day back at school in more than a month and you're going to make us late?" panted Mary as the girls ran toward the Carlton School.

Cassie groaned. "I don't know. I need to learn so much, but the thought of being back in school with only days until vacation ... Shouldn't we go fishing down on the river again instead?"

Mary smiled. "Soon enough. Summer's almost here."

They tumbled through the door of their classroom just as the bell was ringing.

Miss Parker arched her eyebrows. "Well, well," she said. "You girls are gracing us with your presence once more." But she actually looked pleased to see them, perhaps for the first time ever.

Barbara MacKenzie, on the other hand, stuck her tongue out at them as soon as Miss Parker turned her back. Cassie was about to return the favour, but stopped herself. She needed to sit down and focus. She doubted Mrs. Armstrong had ever been distracted by a snob with a violent bully for a brother sticking her tongue out.

At recess time, Cassie and Mary found Barbara reading the paper Freddy sold aloud to her friends. "It's a glorious victory for law and order," she crowed.

"Everyone knows the Committee didn't really win," said Mary. "Your father and his friends just proved how little they care for their workers, and how far they're willing to go. They can't stop progress and they can't keep us down." She was fuming.

Cassie guided her friend gently away from the rich girls. "You're not wrong. I'd bet money on it. But this isn't the time. Just a few days, remember? And then we'll fish and garden and play all summer."

"Maybe," said Mary. "Listen, Cassie. You know I want to spend all summer with you. But there's something else I want to do too. I'm thinking of helping Mrs. Armstrong organize more girls. There are so many who aren't unionized yet. I mean, she'll do the talking. But I know she needs help handing out pamphlets and collecting names. There's a great deal of work to do."

Cassie burst out laughing. "I like this new Mary, you know. Fair enough. Do you think she'd take the help of a raggedy ex-papergirl, too?"

Together, the friends weathered the last of the school year.

* * *

By Sunday, school was over, and the girls were working in the back garden in the sunshine when Billy arrived home from another secret meeting. "Good news, girls," he said. "Mrs. Armstrong is out."

"Already!" said Mary. "That *is* good news. Is she okay? Was she hurt?"

"Apparently she's fine," said Billy. "I heard it from Daniel, who saw Mr. Armstrong just outside his house after he got her yesterday. She's hungry and they didn't treat her well, but she's home safe and that's what counts." He reached over and pulled a plump bean off its vine. "I suppose I'd better get used to this," he said.

"What do you mean?" said Cassie.

"Well, they're not hiring me back on as a policeman. Not right now, and maybe not ever. And the streetcars are starting back up so there's no money in the jitney. I'm going to go out to the country and take farm work. I'll be picking beans all day."

Cassie felt her eyes stinging. She couldn't believe he had to give up policing and go live away from her.

"Cheer up, Cassie. I'll be back by November when the harvest is over. We'll figure it out. You won't even miss me."

* * *

He was wrong about that. Cassie missed her brother desperately. He wrote her two letters a week, telling her how much he loved the fresh country air and how much he hated roosters ("Stupid and mean," he wrote. "Remind me of the Citizens' Committee.")

He sent home money, too. Mr. Hopkins seemed terribly embarrassed about it, but it took him much longer than it took Billy to find work. Day after day he searched, and finally found it washing dishes at the Oxford Hotel, the very hotel where Mrs. Hopkins had been working at the café. He came home every night with his leg aching and his shoulders slumped. It was a step down from his fine work as a police officer, and it was hard on his aging body. Cassie heard the sadness in his voice as he talked to Mrs. Hopkins every night when Cassie was meant to be in bed.

If there was justice coming, it was taking its own sweet time.

EPILOGUE

April 1921

"Come on, Cassie!" called Mary from the back door.

Cassie rushed down the stairs to the kitchen and kissed her mother. "Are you sure you don't want to come?" she asked.

"Quite sure. I've had enough of crowds to last a lifetime," said her mother.

"Fair enough. I'll tell Mrs. Armstrong hello from her favourite biscuit maker."

Mrs. Hopkins blushed as Cassie pulled on her winter coat and ran outside.

The girls linked arms as they hurried down the laneway. Mary came to an abrupt halt, yanking Cassie off balance.

"What are you d —"

"One!" interrupted Mary, pointing to a small patch of earth where the delicate, tightly closed head of a crocus was just emerging from the crusty late-winter snow that lay everywhere.

"Already!" said Cassie. "That has to be a good omen, right?"

"I'd say so." Mary reached down and very gently touched the bud with the tip of her finger. "For luck," she explained as she stood again.

A couple of blocks away, they saw people standing in line.

"Surely, they can't be here for ..." said Cassie.

Mary was beaming. "See? They didn't beat us. We're still strong!"

It was true; the people hadn't been beaten. In fact, George Armstrong, Helen Armstrong's husband, had been elected to the legislature while he was on a prison farm along with five of the other strike leaders.

They had served their sentence in a labour camp ("Don't they see the irony? A labour camp, good grief," Mary had said scathingly), and now they were coming home.

And all these people were there to greet them, bundled in their winter coats and stomping their feet to keep warm against the wind.

"Eighty ... ninety ... there are at least a hundred people on that section of Edmonton Street alone!" said Cassie. They hurried on toward the Armstrongs' house.

"I count a thousand people in that line," said Mary.

As they came to the little house, the rattle and growl of a car carried from farther down the street. Everyone in the line — young, old, women and men, all clearly of the labouring class — stilled. Those on the street stepped aside.

And up to the small Armstrong house pulled a car packed with men.

Just then, the crowd around the Armstrongs' house cleared a little, and Mrs. Armstrong emerged, beaming.

The engine stopped. The doors opened. Six weathered, lean, bearded men emerged from the car.

One cried out and leaped toward Mrs. Armstrong. They embraced and the crowd cheered.

When they pulled apart, Mrs. Armstrong leapt onto a stone by the sidewalk to put her just slightly above the crowd.

"Welcome, everyone! Thank you all so much for coming! Today we celebrate the return of these six men from their unjust incarceration! We also mark the homecoming of our honourable Member of the Legislature, Mr. George Armstrong!"

The joyful cheers of the crowds billowed like sheets on a clothesline, buffeting Cassie and Mary where they stood, spellbound at the energy of the crowd.

They watched as, one by one, the people in the line approached and shook the hand of every returning man.

Cassie took a notebook out of her pocket and scribbled down what she could see. She'd found herself doing this since the strike, wanting to record what she saw going on around her. She'd become used to reading about the day's events in the bulletin every day during the general strike, and ever since, she liked to write down the happenings of the city at night before she went to bed.

She'd even begun trying to turn her thoughts into articles,

and behind her back, Mary had shown two of them to Mrs. Armstrong a few months before. Mrs. Armstrong had written her an encouraging note, telling her that her voice was important and that she'd be writing for the papers one day. It was a startling and exciting thought, the idea of becoming more than just a typewriter girl, even. Becoming more like Mrs. Armstrong.

After about twenty people had filed through, Mrs. Armstrong pulled away from George's side and walked onto the street, fanning her nose. She saw the girls watching and smiled.

"My rabble rouser and my papergirl! How lovely of you to come meet the returning heroes. I hate to tell them, but they stink to high heaven. I'm so happy to see George, but I need a little break! Mary, while I have you, let me ask how things went at the meeting last night."

Cassie smiled as Mary updated Mrs. Armstrong on union business. Mrs. Smith had become one of the most active members of the Women's Labour League, representing textile workers. Mary went to every meeting alongside her, taking notes and talking to the girls closer to her own age than her mother's.

Once they were finished the update, Mrs. Armstrong said, "Girls, I could use your help. Come with me."

They wove their way past the exhausted but happy-looking men and the thousand well-wishers shaking their hands.

"Right here," said Mrs. Armstrong, pausing by a metal barrel. "Can you gather a few twigs and some newspapers and get a nice fire going in here?"

"It is a cold day, isn't it?" said Cassie. "Is this to keep the men warm?"

Mrs. Armstrong smiled ruefully. "Oh goodness, they've been working outside for a year; I'm sure they're warm enough. No, this is so that Mr. Armstrong has somewhere to burn those godawful clothes before he comes back into my house."

As Cassie and Mary laughed, another voice came from behind them.

"What's so funny? You need some help there?"

It was Freddy, with a hat pulled down over his eyes. He had to keep a low profile in this crowd.

Cassie didn't see a lot of Freddy these days. He was busy, still working for the fat cats, still planning to be rich himself one day. Now he was in charge of the paperboys instead of spending his days on the streets. He was making a little more money, and his family was eating a little bit better.

And he was slowly, secretly, working to unionize his paperboys.

Cassie watched as Mary warmly greeted her previous enemy. She watched as Mrs. Armstrong extended her hand to say hello to one of her newest allies. She looked up at the men and women, the boys and girls, waiting on this cold day to greet and thank their heroes, and she felt the strength that came from being with this enormous crowd who all believed in the same thing. She hummed the simple notes of "Solidarity Forever" as she pulled out her notebook again.

Would there ever be justice for all these people? Maybe in her lifetime, and maybe not. But as Cassie recorded this moment in words, observing the passion and determination thrumming through the crowd, she felt another kind of power, one that no one could take from this papergirl.

It was the power of a truth being shared.

AFTERWORD

The 1919 Winnipeg General Strike was one of the most influential strikes in Canadian history and set the groundwork for positive change for workers. It involved thirty thousand workers and inspired sympathy strikes in many Canadian cities, from Amherst, Nova Scotia, all the way to Victoria, British Columbia. Workers around the world were inspired by the strength displayed in Winnipeg. Girls and women played important roles in the strike, but their history has been left out of many accounts of the strike.

The path from the strike to workers' rights wasn't short or straightforward. It took almost three decades after the strike for Canadian workers to win the right to representation by a union and collective bargaining rights. Some say that means the strike wasn't a success.

But others argue that even if the strike didn't meet all its immediate objectives, it served as a powerful source of inspiration — for people a hundred years ago, and for us, a century later. And we can honour the bravery of those thirty thousand workers by continuing to seek labour rights and justice.

A NOTE ON SOURCES

To supplement the research in Melinda McCracken's original manuscript, I turned mainly to primary sources, looking at the archived newspapers in the University of Manitoba's digital collections <https://digitalcollections.lib.umanitoba.ca/islandora/object/uofm%3Amanitobia_newspapers>.

The website of the Manitoba Historical Society provided priceless research and context, including correspondence from A.J. Andrews to Arthur Meighan during the strike itself. I also found a treasure trove of information about Helen Armstrong in the excellent documentary *The Notorious Mrs. Armstrong*, written and directed by Paula Kelly. Along with many details about Helen Armstrong's life and the strike itself, this documentary includes anecdotes about Helen Armstrong taking children to sing at the penitentiary, which I used as inspiration for a chapter in this book, and her burning her husband's clothes after he was released from prison, before she'd let him into their house. Of course, Helen Armstrong and all the other historical figures who appear in this book are fictionalized.

EDUCATIONAL AND
ADDITIONAL RESOURCES

For a teacher/student guide and activities, a photo gallery and other resources related *Papergirl* and the 1919 Winnipeg General Strike, go to <https://fernwoodpublishing.ca/resources/papergirl>.